The Vampyre's Witching Hour

Descent into Darkness

Carley Eason Evans

The Vampyre's Witching Hour

Copyright © 2025

by Carley Eason Evans

All rights reserved.

ISBN: 9798285816089

Whether we fall by ambition, blood, or lust, like diamonds we are cut with our own dust.

John Webster

Prologue

I am Doctor John Polidori. I *was* a surgeon until the unfortunate and horrific events that follow in this book. I was *also* the friend of and personal physician to Lord George Gordon Byron, the famed Romantic poet, during our Grand Tour which formed the completion of our educations.

At the end of the Grand Tour, during our arrival at Villa Diodati near Lake Geneva, my right index finger was bitten by Lord Byron's pet, an exotic Mandrill monkey to be exact. In biting me, the beast transmitted a villainy to my body, a malady of the human soul which is difficult to explain and harder to believe.

Herein is my story.

Chapter One: Mungo

For late spring in Switzerland, the sky was unduly grey. Since early March, rain had been falling incessantly because of the eruption of the volcano, Mount Tambora in Indonesia during the previous April 1815. The ash filled the air so that when the sun was shining, ever so briefly through a thick cloud cover, I suspected that even the forest animals could not feel it. Reflecting the leaden sky above it, the surface of the lake near Geneva was decidedly grey as well. it

By mid May 1816, we had come to the end of the Grand Tour, myself and George Gordon, better known as Lord Byron, and now found ourselves on Lake Geneva in Villa Diodati, a lovely house which Lord Byron had rented for us.

As for myself, I was not only ill, but sullen, tired of Lord Byron's company. I correctly assumed that he was even less enthralled with *my* presence. I *had been* his personal physician as well as his on again, off again friend. Now, he would have preferred that I disappear into the background.

Before our arrival in May, we had traveled to Lake Geneva in a series of coaches. With us, in the luxury coach owned by George, were a dog, a monkey, specifically a male Mandrill, and a peacock. All three creatures were claimed as belonging to Byron, but he paid little heed to them throughout our journey. The coachman took care to feed them and occasionally did speak to the dog. He was less inclined to speak to the Mandrill, and utterly ignored the noisy peacock.

On a particularly dreary day in the coach, the large, colorful monkey was unable to sit still, climbing over my lap, knocking my top hat off my head, picking up my rather expensive umbrella, and poking my ribs with it several times before I walloped the nasty animal across its blue and red nose at which point the beast bit my index finger, causing it to bleed profusely onto my slacks. I wrapped my finger in my white handkerchief, watched my blood spread into the linen fabric, then swore, something I rarely allowed to issue from my lips. I felt the blood rush to my cheeks, and closed my eyes tightly to avoid seeing my embarrassment reflected in George's expression. Lord Byron scolded me, commanded me to leave his animal alone. I protested briefly, then stared out the carriage window to watch the fog as it settled on the passing landscape. I was weary of my companions, especially of the one who was human. I unwrapped the handkerchief to study my finger a few minutes later. The blood was now congealed and the bite mark clearly visible. I hoped that the wound would not turn, as I did not relish losing the finger. *After all, I am a surgeon. As such, I require use of my digits, especially those of my dominant hand.*

"You ought to be more tolerant of Mungo," said George, not looking at me or at the Mandrill.

I glanced at Lord Byron, grunted, returned to perusing the rain and fog.

"He isn't accustomed to being in a carriage," explained my companion. "He just wants to play."

I swallowed my odd tasting saliva, ventured to say, "You play with him then." This shut Lord Byron up as he also grunted, annoyed, then closed his eyes. Mungo leapt onto his chest and with a hairless fist poked George in the gut. The man tried to ignore this behavior, but pushed the monkey from him. Mungo bounced off the floor of the carriage, reached up to hang briefly from a drape arranged on the window nearest me. Mungo screeched in my direction, and the peacock standing on the bench next to George screamed, *may-awe, may-awe.* Lord Byron swatted the bird which retreated to the floor. Mungo jumped down from the drape and rolled around at our feet, sticking out his tongue at various moments. I tried my best to ignore the monkey and the other two animals, including Boomer, George's dog that was asleep next to me on my side of the carriage.

I began to think about what lay ahead for myself and Lord Byron. *How are we going to get through the long, oddly wet and bleak summer? Will I be able to tolerate Mungo and Boomer and the unnamed peacock? Will I be able to avoid a fistfight with George?* An image came to my mind, that of Lord Byron and myself in a hastily constructed boxing ring while both of us wore mud red gloves and nothing but drawers. I was certain George would knock me clean out. I was determined to avoid my imaginary fighting ring whether it turned out to be formal or, more likely, informal. I imagined that I might say something offensive and next thing I would know, George would have knocked my block off. *I would be out cold for a week!*

We arrived at Villa Diodati in the village Cologny the next afternoon, having spent a cold and dreary night in a small establishment along the way. Once at our final destination, George settled into a luxurious suite on the top floor. I took a smaller bedroom on the first floor, close to the expansive kitchen. Our friends had not yet arrived.

As I unpacked my luggage, my index finger began to throb. What I did not know at that time was how George had come to obtain Mungo. While we were traveling together on the Grand Tour, we separated briefly. During this time apart, I did not know that George traveled to central Africa where he purchased Mungo from a dark man along a dirt path. The man was elderly with no hair on the very top of his elongated head except he sported a long grey and black speckled beard. His ebony skin was wrinkled, and his eyes deep set and far apart. Later as we sat in arm chairs around one of the villa's fireplaces, George would confess that the gentleman looked like a skull with skin stretched around it. I would shudder then. At any rate, in Africa, George had purchased Mungo for some odd amount of money, keeping the name the old man told him belonged to the animal.

"Do not change his name, sir," the seller had warned. "Mungo has always been his name, for many years. Always. Never change his name."

And George had promised.

Not knowing any of this information about the Mandrill, I examined the swollen wound on my finger. The edges of the bite marks were red, angry. I felt my forehead, believing I must have a fever. I stripped off my clothing, down to my drawers, and climbed into the large soft bed. I was asleep in seconds, awakening some time later to darkness. *What time had I fallen asleep?* I wondered. *Was it afternoon? Yes, it was before supper when I fell asleep.*

The house was quiet and I thought that it must be the middle of the night. Indeed it was about two in the morning. I stretched out again, ignoring the throbbing in my hand, and tried to sleep. When I awoke just after sunrise, my hand was painfully swollen. My throat was excruciatingly dry and my tongue was stuck to the roof of my mouth. I tried to rise, but felt weak all over. Fear overtook me as I imagined what might reside in Mungo's saliva.

A half hour later, I heard the bell calling the house to breakfast. I struggled but managed to rise from the bed, wash my body sufficiently at the washstand, awkwardly dress, then walk slowly to the dining room where I sat at the long mahogany table. A tall middle aged woman wearing a standard waitstaff uniform greeted me and served me a small cup of coffee. I drank it black, draining the cup almost immediately. I looked for a second cup, but she had disappeared back into the kitchen.

At that moment, Lord Byron entered the dining room. I noted that he considered whether he might sit at the far end rather than with me. With a slight shake of his head, he proceeded to sit across from me at the lengthy rectangular table. Without looking at me, George said, "Good morning, Polly Dolly."

"Excuse me?"

"Good morning," said George omitting the diminutive, nay insulting name he had given to me.

"Good morning, George," I responded. "How did you sleep?"

"Very well indeed," he said. He did not ask me how I slept, so I looked for the second cup of coffee. I waited patiently until the same woman appeared to bring Lord Byron his coffee. I said to her, "May I have another, please."

She smiled at me, most of her teeth missing. "Certainly, sir." Then she stopped, staring at my hand which I had laid gently on the bare mahogany table to the right of my plate. "Oh my," she whispered, then crossed herself as we Catholics do. When she crossed her heart, I felt a strong aversion to the woman which I did not understand.

Lord Byron looked at the shocked woman, asked, "What?"

"His hand, sir. Look at his hand," she whispered hoarsely.

We each looked at my right hand. The hand, which I then realized I could no longer feel, was black. The nails had grown long and ragged. They were a dark purple. Little tuffs of black hair grew out of each knuckle on each finger. I screeched out a guttural exclamation of horror then fainted dead away.

✝

When I woke, I realized I was in a storage room off the kitchen. I lay on a hard wooden table while a doctor examined me. Lord Byron was not present. Neither was the waitstaff, the woman who had crossed herself.

"Be still," the physician commanded. Then he asked me what had caused this unusual ailment.

"I was bitten by that monkey of Lord Byron's."

"A monkey here at Diodati?"

"Yes, in the carriage. What? A few days ago, I believe," realizing *I have lost time.*

"This is a strange malady indeed," mused the doctor. Then he smiled softly, said, "I am sorry. Please forgive me. My name is Doctor Hollifield. I understand you are a physician as well."

I nodded. "I am." I sighed, "Nice to make your acquaintance, Doctor Hollifield."

"Hmm," he mused. "I am afraid you may lose this hand, Doctor Polidori."

I gasped, and fainted again. I was twenty years old and recently had earned my degree in medicine from the University of Edinburgh. Lord Byron was my first patient and he was never, *well hardly ever ill.* I usually treated his hangovers while providing companionship during the Grand Tour. Now I would lose my hand and my livelihood. As darkness swam toward me, I thought *I am doomed to a life I will not relish.*

When I became conscious again, my hand was wrapped in multiple layers of white gauze. *I have my hand.* As if he could read my mind, Doctor Hollifield said, "Not for long, Doctor Polidori. Not for long." He shook his head, added, "Else you will die."

I could hear his heart beating in his chest. *How odd.* I smelled his blood pumping through the veins in his arms, in his body underneath his lab coat and shirt. I began to drool. I wiped my mouth and chin with my left hand after momentarily attempting to use my cocooned right hand. I sucked and swallowed, but my saliva was out of control and oddly thick and foul tasting. I felt strong, inordinately. I said, "Come here, doctor." My voice boomed in the small room. The man turned, stared at me. He stepped toward me. I sat straight up on the table, swung my legs over the edge, and reached out. The doctor walked into my arms. He turned his head to the left, his neck bare above his white collar. I leapt at him, sunk my teeth into the man's carotid artery, began to rapidly drink his blood even as I thought, *How disgusting.*

Sank 12

Within moments, I had drained the good doctor's body of all its life giving sustenance. I sat down on the table again, letting the doctor crumple to the floor. I presumed that he was dead, and he was. I had killed a man. I shook my head, realizing I felt better than I had in a long time. Stronger, smarter, older than my twenty years. I thought of Mungo.

A moment later, Mungo scratched at the window behind me. *Come in, Mungo. Come on in, and take care of this.*

The Mandrill worked the latch on the window until he managed to open it. He climbed in, jumped down, grabbed an arm and leg of the dead man, began to drag the limp body across the cold tile floor, leaving a trail of translucence, a liquid slick and shiny. The strong Mungo stuffed the man into a large and open cupboard, pushing and pushing until the doctor fit. The monkey shut the cupboard door and looked at me expectantly. I praised Mungo, then thought, *Leave me now.* The animal obeyed, exiting through the still open window.

As I sat on the edge of the wooden table, I quite unexpectedly felt shame. Only a moment before, I had been exhilarated, feeling powerful, completely in control of myself with the exception of my incomprehensible drooling. Now, I cringed at the memory of drinking a man's blood, of draining a man to the point of his death. Not only this, but I had murdered a fellow physician, a doctor attempting to help me. I was utterly ashamed of myself. I began to weep, then sob uncontrollably.

The door to the storage room swung open. George stood in the door frame. When he saw me crying like an infant, he said, "What is wrong with you, Polly Dolly?" He looked around, asked, "Where is the good doctor, Hollifield?"

"Who?" I asked as innocently as I could manage.

"The doctor I called for you," said an exasperated George.

"He must have left," I lied.

"Without amputating your hand?"

I looked at my bandaged appendage, said, "I think he decided to give it a few days."

"That's not what he told me," protested Lord Byron, puffing out his chest.

"I talked him out of it," I lied again.

"Well, Polly Dolly, that is just stupid."

"Do not call me *that*, George."

"Call you what?"

"That name," I said.

"What name?"

"You know."

"I know what?"

I sighed. I stood up from the table, and pushed past Lord Byron. From somewhere outside, we heard Mungo hooting and the peacock's answering, *may-awe, may-awe*. Boomer began to howl as well.

George looked annoyed. "What is with those creatures?" I turned, glared at him. He grinned at me, mocked, "What?" I gently bit my tongue tip, determined not to respond. George persisted, "What is it, Polly Dolly? Finding yourself speechless?"

When he was not looking at me, I opened my lips to reveal my sharp and now retracted incisors, tasting blood on them. I grinned, then closed my mouth, walked through the kitchen, down the hallway to the broad foyer, then out the front door of the house. The sky was grey with a hint of the sun outlined in a pale yellow despite a steady rain. I could not feel any warmth for the slight sunshine, but my bare left hand began to tingle. It was not unpleasant, nevertheless, I put that hand in a pocket of my slacks. My face tingled as well, but I ignored the sensation. Once I reached the line of trees, with protection from both the sun and the steady rain, the sensation dissipated. I was completely comfortable again.

Mungo appeared from the underbrush. The monkey stared at me with anticipation, as if to ask *what's next?*

Chapter Two: Reflection

I discovered over the next three days that my consumption of Doctor Hollifield's blood was sustaining. The hunger I had experienced when I first became aware of the man's heartbeat and the smell of his life was satisfied. I did not need to eat, drink again, at least not during those first days at the house.

On the fourth day, I commanded Mungo to catch a wild rabbit for me to snack upon. I was gratified that the blood of this rain soaked little animal helped assuage the beginnings of my thirst. I relaxed and awaited the arrival of our guests.

My right hand was still bandaged and I had not ventured to look upon it. Whatever poison from the Mandrill's bite that was seeping into my bloodstream apparently was not going to kill me. I wondered if I might be immortal. *Perhaps I cannot die.* I did not understand why I thought this might be possible, but in the recesses of my mind, I began to believe that *nothing can kill me.* I grinned at this thought.

On the fifth afternoon of our stay, Lord Byron's guests began to arrive. First to come into the villa were Percy Bysshe Shelley and Mary Wollstonecraft Godwin. Percy was twenty and three years old whereas Mary was approaching her nineteenth birthday in August of that summer. These two were known to be lovers, owned a house nearby, and both were more friends to Lord Byron than they were to me. At twenty, I was the youngest of the men, and the one without a lover.

George, who was the oldest of us at the ripe age of twenty and eight years, greeted his friends warmly, and was especially attentive to the very young Miss Godwin. He bellowed, "Welcome, welcome, welcome my dear sweet Mary." He turned to her male companion, clapped the considerably shorter man on his left shoulder, said loudly, "Hello, hello, dear Percy. Hello."

"Hello, George," said Mary, smiling.

"We would like to be shown to our bedroom," said Percy, "if you do not mind."

"Oh," I said, "of course you would." I strolled forward from the place where I had been leaning against the wall of the foyer. I picked up Percy's large luggage piece with the intention of starting off down the hallway toward the kitchen. "I believe you both are down this way, close to my bedroom."

Lord Byron interrupted. "No, no, no, Polly Dolly. Mary and Percy each have rooms on the top floor on either side of my suite." And he roughly took the suitcase from my left hand, and moved toward the central staircase. He put the luggage down, whistled quite shrilly for a bellboy who appeared several moments later. With apparent impatience, George commanded the young man, "Take these cases to either of the bedrooms next to mine."

"Yes, sir," said the boy, realizing he would need to make several trips up and down the staircase. He looked at Lord Byron who sharply repeated his command. Startled, the young man jumped, grabbed the first luggage piece and began to trudge up the stairs. "That is a good lad," said the Lord. Byron who turned to Mary, hooked his arm around her tiny waist to pull her to his side. "Come, Mary, let us have an afternoon brandy." He glanced at Percy, then briefly at me. "Let us all have a brandy, shall we?"

A clap of thunder, then a harder rain began outside. Ignoring the weather, we strolled into the rather small living area, sat down. Mary and George sat together on a short sofa that seemed to swallow them. Percy took his seat in a matching armchair while I sat in a straight backed chair with a wicker seat after first picking it up to move it closer to the sofa. I looked at Percy as I sat down. Mary smiled at me, said, "So I understand you are now a doctor, John."

"Yes," I said, "that is true."

"And a surgeon," she added.

"Yes, I was indeed trained in surgical techniques."

"Polly Dolly," said George, "is not likely to be participating in surgery, however."

Percy chuckled ever so softly, but Mary seemed to think before speaking, deciding I thought that she ought to ignore George's odd and rather mean way of naming me. She asked, "Oh, why is that?"

I lifted my bandaged right hand, explained, "George's monkey bit me. Doctor Hollifield thinks perhaps my hand will need amputating, to save my life."

"Oh dear God," said Mary. "How dreadful."

Percy ventured, "Where *is* the good doctor?"

"Bugger disappeared," said George.

"Well," said Mary, "that was rude."

I blushed, then said, "Yes, I suppose it was. But I figure he had an emergency. He probably will return in a day or two."

"You might be dead in a day or two," offered Lord Byron. He looked around. "Where *is* that damned woman? I want my brandy."

"Claire should be here soon," said Mary, standing up and walking over to Percy. She sat quite daintily upon his lap, crossing her bare ankles which appeared ever so slightly below her skirt. "We ought to wait for her."

I asked, "Claire? She is your stepsister, correct?"

"Yes, my dearest companion," confessed Mary.

"Then," I continued, "we definitely should wait on Claire's arrival. When do you expect her?"

"Soon," offered Percy, patting Mary's gloved hands which she had folded in her lap.

Lord Byron stood, paced to the fireplace. "Well, you three can wait for Miss Claire Clairmont. I am having a brandy now." At this, he strolled from the room, heading presumably toward the kitchen to find someone, anyone to fetch him a liquor.

Thunder clapped again and a flash of lightning appeared outside the main window of the small room. "I am afraid we are in for a wet, dreary summer," I said.

"That damned volcano," said Percy.

Mary stood, took one step in my direction. "May I look at your hand, John?"

I instinctively hid my heavily bandaged right hand in the pocket of my suit jacket. "Oh, that is not necessary."

Percy gently scolded Mary who blushed. "I am sorry John. My curiosity is notorious."

"Yes," I said, "I have heard. Your curiosity and your imagination are both well known."

Mary blushed again. She returned to sit on Percy's lap, but he shifted. Mary rose to sit on the sofa. I thought she may have glared at Percy, but my impression may have been due to my own rather active imagination.

The front door to the villa opened. A drenched yet beautiful young woman entered. The coachman carried her two luggage pieces into the foyer, set them down. The girl tipped the man. "Thank you, miss," he said, tipped his cap, and departed. Mary had left the sofa, and now was hugging Claire.

Claire said, "Dreadful day, is it not?"

I approached our friend, took her hand in my left, kissed it, and playfully spoke with a grave formality, "Good afternoon, Miss Clairmont. Welcome to Villa Diodati." Her natural scent was powerful and I momentarily salivated as I had with Doctor Hollifield. Afraid and embarrassed, I stepped away from the young woman and turned to face the wall at which time I wiped my mouth with a handkerchief, stuffing it into a pocket before turning back to cautiously smile at Claire.

"Why thank you, John. Good to see you again."

"We are about to have brandies," said Mary. "Come and sit with us."

"Oh my goodness," said Claire. "I must dry off first. Which is my room?"

Percy, who had come into the foyer, remarked, "Apparently only George knows."

"Oh," said Claire with excitement, "where is the great poet, Lord Byron?"

"Getting his brandy, we think," I said.

We chuckled as a group, then stood in comfortable silence before Mary suggested we find the kitchen. "George must be there, don't you suppose, John?"

I nodded. We walked down the hallway past the door to my room, and entered the large kitchen. Lord Byron stood by a long wooden table, sipping directly from a bottle of brandy. He turned, grinned. "The brandy is very good. Have some."

Claire said, "Dear George. Which of the bedrooms is mine?"

I offered, "Claire wishes to dry off before having her brandy, George."

"Okay, Polly Dolly." Then Lord Byron spoke to Claire, "So good to have you here this summer. Your room is on the upper floor next to Percy or maybe next to Mary." And he whistled. Claire winced, stepped back. George apologized, "I am dreadfully sorry dear. I do not know how else to call that damn bellboy."

Claire smiled, leaned toward me, and whispered, "Why did George call you that?"

I whispered back, "Honestly, I think he just has decided to be mean."

"Mean?" Claire looked at me with utter disbelief as if Lord Byron could not possibly have a mean streak. "No, really, John. Why is George calling you Polly Dolly? Is this a private joke?"

I decided to be generous, smiled, nodded. "Yes, a private joke." Once again, her scent stunned me, and I was afraid I might do violence against her in front of our mutual friends. I stepped away. "Excuse me." I walked from the kitchen, found my bedroom, entered, shut, and locked the door. I stood in the dim light, breathed deeply several times. Then I sat on the edge of the bed, placed my head between my knees to wait for the thirst, the hunger to subside, but it did not lessen. I wondered, *What is wrong with me?*

Mungo.

The monkey appeared at the window to my room. I rose, unlatched the small aperture, and allowed the very wet stinky animal to enter. I thought, *Another rabbit or perhaps a fawn.*

Mungo hooted, clapped his hands together, leapt through the open window to disappear into the rain and fog.

Thirty and five minutes later, Mungo appeared with a rain soaked, mangled rabbit which he laid at my feet. I picked up the dead thing and sunk my extended incisors into its furry neck, sucked every drop of blood from its limp body. *Take it away now*

Mungo. And, more importantly, make certain you remove Doctor Hollifield's body from the cupboard. He must not be found.

The Mandrill nodded, clapping his hands together, and obeyed me. Where the monkey put the good doctor, I would never know.

I rose, looked in the dressing mirror in an effort to wash my face and rinse out my bloody mouth with water from the washbasin on the nearby washstand, but my reflection was missing. I startled, stepping away from the mirror that showed only the contents of the room behind me. I reached out and touched the surface of the glass with my left hand. *Yes, the mirror is there. Yet, my face is missing.* My first thought was, *How is this unnatural thing possible?* Then, *How many mirrors are in this villa? Where are they? How do I avoid them?* I stepped back again, sat on the edge of the bed. I waited for the blood from the small rabbit to quench my thirst. The feeling of power that I had after killing the doctor did not return, but the hunger subsided.

I flexed my right hand under the gauze cocoon, began to unravel it so as to examine my appendage in privacy. Once I removed the bandage, I saw that the marks of Mungo's bite had completely disappeared. However, my hand remained pitch black and my nails were now an even darker purple, so dark they were almost black. The hair on my knuckles was now coarse and longer than before. I noted that the blackness of my skin had begun to creep toward my wrist as if it was growing. I shuddered. I wrapped my right hand and wrist with clean gauze I carried with me in my medical bag.

I reached up to feel my teeth. The now retracted incisors presently did not seem unduly long or sharp. Yet, I determined that I must neither smile broadly at anyone nor laugh heartily at any joke less my unusual teeth elicit questions I could not answer.

When I returned to the kitchen, the small group of friends was laughing. Byron had distributed the brandy to each person. He queried, "So what are we to do with this horrid summer?"

I interjected, "We might tell each other stories."

"Stories?" George seemed incredulous.

"Yes," cried Mary, quite excited. "We can tell ghost stories."

"We can have a contest," I offered.

"Yes," said Percy. "That is a grand idea. Let us see who among us can compose the best occult tale."

Mary laughed, "I vote we start right away."

Lord Byron frowned, glared at me, groaned to the group, "That is not exactly what I had in mind."

Everyone chuckled, everyone except George and myself.

Chapter Three: Hunger

We did not start right away on storytelling. Lord Byron was determined to derail or if not derail at least delay the contest proposed by the other members of our group. At least, I suspected that he did not want a contest among his friends and against his former physician.

The month of May slid by, seemingly every day more boring and drearier than the next with heavy cloud cover and always at least a light rain. Now and then, thunderstorms rolled in, usually at night. The constant humidity was unbearable, especially for Claire and Mary who complained about their hairdos. Claire repeatedly stated that her hair would not hold "any curls at all." Mary claimed she had given up, saying, "Who cares? Who is going to see me except you four?"

✝

My unabated hunger or thirst, I was not certain which described it best, continued to be satisfied to some extent by Mungo's offerings of squirrels, rabbits, chipmunks, an occasional bird, and finally, a fawn each of which I took in the forest, far away from the villa. There, in the rain and amongst the underbrush, I would bite the animal's neck and suck all its blood from its dead body. *Something is lacking.* Only later would I realize that obviously life is what is missing when creatures are dead. *The blood of the dead is not equivalent to that of the living.*

My long walks, sometimes in a driving rainfall, eventually drew suspicion from the two young women. Claire asked me at breakfast one morning in early June, "Where do you go for so long in the rain, John? What is there to see in that forest day after day?"

I lied, "I walk around Lake Geneva for my daily constitution."

"I did not realize it would take that long to walk around our lake," mused Percy.

George said, "I did not realize Polly Dolly liked rain."

Ignoring Lord Byron, I lied again to Percy, "I take my time."

Mary protested while cutting into her softly boiled egg with a spoon, "Never mind the rain! I am ready to tell my story. I have been working on it since the day we first talked about our contest."

Percy nodded, said, "As you know, dear, I have been writing snatches of poetry, some of it a tad gothic."

I sighed, added, "Yes, I have been writing too. What else is there to do here?"

"Other than walk around Lake Geneva in the rain," offered Mary.

"Well," boomed Byron, "I *always* am writing. Everyone knows that."

"So, let's start," declared Percy.

"Tonight?" I suggested.

Together, all, except myself and George, repeated, "Tonight."

✝

That evening, while the rain continued to pour outside, we sat around the fireplace in the small living area of the large villa. Percy and now and then George poked the logs so that the embers sparked and the flames licked the wood in new spots. We needed the fire as summer 1816 was proving to be the coldest summer of Switzerland's history, known history, that is. Even before the end of that year, 1816 would come to be known as *the year without a summer.*

"I will start," said Mary, clearing her throat. "First, my tale is about a mad scientist who desires to harness lightning…" At that very moment, thunder rumbled, shaking the villa. A flash of lightning was seen outside the main window. Mary laughed, then continued, "So, my mad scientist harnesses the electric current in lightning to bring to life a body that he has created out of various dead men." She stopped, looked for reactions in our faces.

"Wait," said Claire. "You mean to say, this scientist robs graves?"

"Yes, exactly," Mary responded. "He hires grave robbers to locate corpses for his experiment. He selects different body parts and sews them together into a new body. Then he harvests the perfect brain, or so he believes, from another body. He uses a lightning bolt to bring this creation to life. I have it all worked out, well, most of it."

"Oh, that *is* intriguing," said Claire, excited.

"But," I said, "I thought you were supposed to *tell* us the story not tell us *about* the story."

"Yes, sorry, John," lamented Mary. "You are correct, but it is already so long, I am not sure how to begin to tell the tale. Do you have a story?"

"I do," I admitted, "but I still am working on it."

George groaned. "Well, I have a poem to recite."

Everyone laughed.

As we sat around the fireplace listening to Lord Byron's lengthy poem, I became aware that I was hungry. I had attempted to not sit near Claire but through several shifts in the seating arrangement, she wound up next to me. Late in the evening, she leaned in, brushed my left arm, and I heard her heart beating behind her breasts. I thought I would faint, the thirst or hunger was so intense, I could barely resist. I stood up, so abruptly that

Claire's right arm was struck by my left knee. "Ouch," she said, "watch it, John."

I did not even apologize, but rushed from the living area, literally running down the hallway to my bedroom where I entered, locked the door, and crumpled with hunger pangs to the floor. *Mungo.* The monkey did not come. *Mungo.* Once again, the monkey did not appear at the window. I grew concerned. When Mungo did not arrive the third time, I panicked. I began to shake as I imagined biting the soft neck of Claire. I wanted her blood. I craved her blood. *There is nothing I can do. I am going to take her, sooner than later.*

Chapter Four: Claire

As our group was informed later, Mary Godwin repeatedly knocked on the wooden door of Claire's villa bedroom the next morning. When her friend did not respond, Mary located the bellboy, begged him to open the locked door. When he protested, she insisted. Finally, the young man retrieved the key to open the door. Mary entered cautiously. The bellboy hung back, waiting anxiously in the hallway.

Claire lay on the bed atop the coverlet. Her head was turned away from Mary so that her face and neck were obscured. Mary whispered, "Claire?"

Claire groaned softly.

"Claire," said Mary, insistent. "Are you all right?"

Claire rolled over toward Mary's voice. She whispered hoarsely, "I am not sure. I feel so odd."

Mary went to the window, pulled open the heavy drapes. Ambient light poured in, light from behind thick cloud cover. Rain continued to fall. Mary turned to look at her friend. Claire was utterly pale, her skin completely without color. "Oh my God," said Mary. "What has happened to you?"

Claire tried to sit up, but found she could not move. "I do not know. Oh Mary, I am frightened. I have had such horrible dreams."

"From my story?"

"No, no, not from your tale. From something else, something darker."

"Darker than body snatching?"

"Yes, darker." Claire touched a sore area on her neck and her hand came away with flecks of dried blood. She stared at her fingers. "What is this? Oh Mary, what is this? Is this blood?"

Mary examined Claire's hand and then her friend's neck. Dried blood was caked around two small wounds, so small that they were barely visible beneath the dried blood smear. "Yes, Claire, I think that *is* blood. But, where did it come from?"

Claire groaned, then with anger said, "That nasty monkey. It bit John and now, it has bitten me!"

Mary thought about this, then agreed. "It seems so."

"What are we to do?"

"Tell George to get rid of that Mandrill, that is what."

✝

What neither Mary nor Claire knew was that Mungo had been caught and caged on the previous day by Lord Byron. The kitchen help, early in our stay, had complained to George that the Mandrill stole bananas and mangos and other fruits from the pantry. George's solution was to lock up the animal. This was the reason Mungo had not responded to my calls when I finally had given in to my desire to attack Claire for her blood.

✝

I had waited until the house was asleep. While I crept through the villa in darkness, I discovered that I was able to transform into a heavy mist and seep under any door jamb, and on the other side, reconstitute myself in human form. The first few transformations had been disorienting, to say the least. I still am not certain how I managed this feat, but I did. I believe it was a matter of will power. I had to get into Claire's room quietly and turning myself into an insect like a spider or a roach was not a pleasant thought, so I picked a mist, something akin to the fog outside the villa. Once I had seeped into the room, I rose up as a man, and approached the sleeping form. Claire lay on her back, quietly snoring. I leaned down and opened her gown at her neck. The thirst was exponential in its intensity. I nearly spoke. Gently, I leaned down and kissed her lips first, then moved to her neck while salivating *like a dog in heat.* I bit her and instinctively sucked the blood from her jugular vein so as to better control the flow of blood, then forced myself to stop, fearful I might kill her as I had killed the good Doctor Hollifield. *I must not kill Claire. I must not.* With great resolve, I withdrew from her room, once more changing to a heavy mist, leaving under the door in the same way as I had entered.

The next morning, I woke refreshed, feeling much better than I had during these final days of June. I noted that the cloud cover was heavier than it had been and this pleased me for even the scattered light of the sun, the few times it showed itself, had begun to burn in a way I feared.

My first thoughts as I rose were *I hope Claire is alive. I hope she is well enough to make an appearance this morning.*

✝

Claire and Mary were delayed, but both showed for our breakfast. When Claire entered the dining room, Percy gasped. I turned to look at my young victim. She was pale as a new moon and weak as a newborn kitten. Mary supported her as she guided her friend to the closest chair at the table. Claire collapsed into it as Lord Byron pulled it out for her. *George can be charming, even kind,* I mused. I chuckled softly, keeping my lips closed around my now retracted teeth.

Mary looked at me as if to ask what I could possibly be laughing about. I shrugged my shoulders and went back to my eggs. I then noticed I was weary of human foodstuff, none of which had any flavor I wanted. *Nothing tastes so good as human blood, blood, that is, from a living human being.* I pushed the soft, disgusting egg around in my mouth, and finally managed to swallow it. I gagged. Percy looked at me, puzzled. Again, I shrugged my shoulders, said, "Eggshell."

"Oh dear," said Mary.

"Nothing to worry over," I assured her.

Mary turned her attention to the ailing Claire who was so weak, she was unable to feed herself. "I believe she needs a physician." Then Mary softly gasped, looked at me. "Oh John, I forgot. You *are* a physician!"

Keeping my lips closed, I chuckled again. "Yes, I am." I stood up, walked around the table. I touched Claire's forehead. She startled, shuddered.

Mary alarmed, asked, "What is wrong?"

Claire whispered, "A strong chill went through me."

"You have a fever, Claire," I said. "You should eat what you can, drink some more water, go back to bed. I will check on you later to see if your fever has broken."

"Yes," she said. "Thank you, John."

"My utmost pleasure, Claire," I said, smiling again with my lips closed tightly against my teeth.

✝

Several days later, Claire had regained most of her strength. She liked to sit outside on the brick entrance to the villa. The bellboy whose name not one of us knew provided a rocking chair for Claire to sit in. He also found a large woolen shawl to throw over the young woman's lap and legs.

"Chilly out here, miss," he said. "Best to keep warm."

✝

In early summer, around Lake Geneva, it should not have been as cold as it was that virtually absent season. The darkness in the sky was a bother to everyone but myself. I welcomed the clouds which kept the hidden sun from burning my skin.

At night, gathered around the fireplace, we had begun to tell our stories. Mary titled her tale, *Frankenstein* and we were delighted to hear what she had created, what she was creating. The monster was sympathetic, tragic, and we loved hearing about him. I leaned forward with eagerness as Mary told her story.

My tale I had titled *The Vampyre* and it was, admittedly, a tad close to the truth of my situation. But I was careful when I told it to the group. Byron kept calling me "Polly Dolly" and no one protested. I decided to let his insult go as in several recent dreams I had had visions of my eventual revenge.

Percy recited snatches of poems he kept revising. Lord Byron pontificated through his lengthy poetry offerings, if I am to remain honest. We listened nevertheless and applauded his works as he *was* the most successful and famous of our lot.

✝

By mid June, the thirst, the hunger came again, unbidden and undeniable. One night, I surrendered to this blood lust, crept as heavy mist into Claire's room and bit her again, once more taking my sustenance from her jugular vein. I drank as much as I dared. Then I stretched out beside her and stared at the ceiling, thinking I might bite her once more before leaving. I waited, held my breath. I briefly argued with myself. Then I leaned in, took Claire in my arms, bit her neck sharply. She cried out, opened her eyes. I clapped my left hand over her mouth as she attempted to scream. She shook her head, then clawed at my chest and arms. She struggled as I drained more blood from her. Finally, she succumbed to overwhelming weakness, losing consciousness.

I remained at her side after forcing myself to stop drinking her blood. I rested for several hours before slinking out the same way I came in. As I moved as mist, I felt more like animal than man.

Yet, the next morning, I again felt better than I had since biting the young girl the first time. As before, Claire was discovered in her bed by Mary, who shrieked because this time her friend appeared to be near death. We all came running. As the physician, I examined Claire, sighed, admitted, "I am not sure what is wrong with her."

"We should take her to hospital," said Percy.

Mary nodded. Lord Byron agreed. I agreed as well. *If I protest, no one in our group will understand my reluctance.*

So, Claire was taken by horse drawn ambulance to hospital in nearby Clarens where she was admitted to a bed in a large ward. Within a few hours, the doctors there decided to perform a bloodletting procedure on her with leeches. This bloodletting practice I did protest, vehemently. But they easily convinced Lord Byron that I was wrong and they were right. Claire nearly died that very day. I was desperate to keep her alive as her blood was intoxicating, and she was my one and only source of nourishment.

When I first saw the black ugly and squishy creatures on Claire's arms and upper chest, I flinched. As the leeches extracted blood from her, she grew weaker and showed even less color than she had after the times that I had taken blood from the jugular vein in her neck. I sat down beside her bed, realizing that I was a leech. *I am a giant ugly leech sucking away this young woman's life.* I groaned as I remembered that the Mandrill, Mungo was still locked in a wire cage and I had not been able to convince George to release the poor animal. I was trapped for the moment. Claire's blood scent was irresistible and I convinced myself that I had no alternative.

As Claire grew weaker rather than stronger over the first hour of bloodletting, I took Lord Byron aside. I talked to him in the hallway outside Claire's hospital ward. He did not see reason, so I spoke with Percy, begged him to intervene. Percy understood and was able to convince George to see reason and agree to remove Claire from the care of the quack physicians, and allow his previous personal physician to take on the care of Claire back at the villa.

I then spoke with Percy rather than Byron. I told him, "She will be better off, Percy. Trust me."

Percy took my arm, said, "I do, John. I do trust you."

"Unfortunately," I commented, "it seems that Lord Byron does not trust me."

✝

Back at Villa Diodati, in my bedroom, I lectured myself, sternly telling myself in no uncertain terms that *I must not take blood from Claire again, at least not any time soon.* Then I whispered with new conviction, *No, never again. I will not be a leech on Claire.*

Chapter Five: George

Once I decided to leave Claire alone, I had to find a new source of food. The logical choice was George Gordon, a man who once I had called my friend even as I functioned as his personal physician during the Grand Tour, the final phase of our educations. Our falling out, which had begun in April and May, was in completion during our June and July stay at Villa Diodati. Our conflict was primarily the result of George's inexplicable decision to mock my surname by calling me "Polly Dolly."

Granted, this change in his demeanor toward me occurred before the women came to the villa, but intensified with their arrival. Lord Byron's interest in flirting with Mary, who was obviously Percy's love interest, disturbed me. But his attraction to Claire strained our relationship even more. Apparently, both George and I had fallen for Claire although for markedly different reasons. I craved the young girl for the unique scent and taste of her blood. George loved the young girl because he lusted after her luscious body. We clashed often that summer. By late June, I had decided to pursue the blood of my former friend and client.

I waited until a particularly dark night, sliding up the main staircase as a slow, floating mist, entering his luxurious suite under the door jamb, gliding across the rug placed atop the hardwood floor, and up onto the man's large bed. Lord Byron slept soundly. I knew this from months of travel with him. He snored loudly and stopped breathing occasionally. I lingered as grey mist beside him, making certain he was fully asleep, completely unaware of my presence. Then I transformed from mist into myself, stretched out beside him, waiting patiently. I was not especially hungry or thirsty that night, but I knew that as soon as I began, I would find it difficult to stop feeding. I turned onto my side and slipped my right hand, still bandaged, under Lord Byron's chest, resting it below the small of his back. He

torso

shifted, groaned. I leaned in, pulled his silk sleeping jacket away from his neck, and struck. I bit through his skin and muscle into his jugular vein, then began to suck, his blood flowing into me. George's blood had an odd taste to it, but I ignored its slightly unpleasant quality and continued to feed. I thought *maybe I will kill him*, but resisted the urge to switch to his carotid artery, knowing I would need him alive. I stopped, wiping my mouth on my sleeve. I rolled off the bed, moved across the floor again as mist. I left George sleeping as I had found him.

Again, in the morning, I felt renewed, strengthened, and powerful. At breakfast, a weakened George stumbled in, demanding the house's "strongest coffee." As he waited for his coffee, Lord Byron looked at me, stared at my bandaged right hand, and remarked, "Why is your hand still wrapped up in gauze? Has it never healed?" And he glared at me with such derision that I blushed. He continued, "You ought to be dead by now, Polly Dolly."

"Stop calling me that," I spat. I was angry and my rage surprised me and the entire company at our table. Everyone looked at me with momentary displeasure.

George spat in return, "Why should I?"

"Because my surname is Polidori," I said. Mary, Claire, and even Percy nodded approval, but quickly returned to their breakfasts.

Lord Byron smirked, said, "No, your name at Diodati is Polly Dolly. I will always call you Polly Dolly, and there is *not* a thing you can do about it." He leaned back and put his hands behind his head. He smiled at me, a huge grin. A spot of dried blood was on his collar.

I remarked, "I think your Mandrill has bitten you, Lord Byron."

George shook his head, said, "Mungo is still caged."

"Maybe so," I said. "Maybe not."

Mary looked at George, said, "Well, something has bitten you."

"What?"

"There," she said, "just above your collar, George, my God, I see what looks to be a small bite mark."

Claire moaned, whispered, "Not again." No one other than myself took notice of her disturbing remark.

Lord Byron repeated himself, "Mungo could not possibly be the animal that bit me." Then he felt his neck, a spot that definitely appeared tender in response to his touch.

"Well," I ventured, "some sort of animal is running about the villa at night biting people."

Percy remarked, "Sounds like your vampyre story, John."

"It does, doesn't it?" I said. "But, of course, there is no such thing."

"Of course there is not!" said Mary.

We all nodded, looking at each other.

"Lock your doors, ladies," said George, then he grinned.

Claire spoke quietly with a dark emphasis I could not miss, "I am going to wear a cross, a crucifix around my neck from this moment forward."

✝

The next day, Lord Byron directed his coachman to take Claire into Clarens so that she might purchase a silver crucifix and chain. Mary Godwin remarked to me that this behavior was extremely odd in that "Claire is not in the least bit religious."

"Then," I mused, "I doubt that crucifix will help."

"Whatever do you mean?"

"I mean that in order to have any power over the dark forces of this world, faith is required."

Mary raised her eyebrows, and bit her lower lip likely harder than she intended. She drew a tiny drop of blood. When its scent reached me, I was shocked at my response. I nearly leapt at my young friend. As she stepped back from me, Mary's eyes widened and she asked, "Are you all right, John?"

"I am," I lied. "I need to rest. I have not been sleeping well."

"In that case, take a long afternoon siesta."

"I will," I lied again. Instead of retiring to my room, I walked down the hallway, through the kitchen, out the back entrance and into the forest despite a heavy rain. Eventually, I located the first snare that I had awkwardly fashioned earlier that week. It was empty. I had not yet trapped a rabbit or even a field mouse. *Nothing.* I moved on to a second one, and this too was empty. I sighed, returned to the villa. Mary, standing in the doorway near the brick slab situated just outside the back entrance, spied me returning from the edge of the woods. She waved, smiling weakly, looking puzzled. Then she turned and disappeared into the depth of the villa's kitchen. I continued to my room where, after toweling off, I struggled to sleep.

That night I woke, but resisted going into George's room to feed. I was concerned that suspicions had been raised, especially with Claire. She seemed to know instinctively that *something evil* resided in me.

The next morning, the shiny silver cross with the crucified man hanging on it was around her neck. She kept stroking it throughout her morning meal. This caused in me an aversion that I once again did not understand. All I recognized was that the crucifix repulsed me.

†

After that morning, our daily lives essentially returned to normal. Claire was never without the crucifix around her neck and I discovered quite by accident that I could not approach her beyond several inches. I could come up to Claire, but if I attempted to touch her, my hand was repelled. No one seemed to notice that my hand was pushed away from this young woman except perhaps Claire herself.

The repulsion happened as I said quite by accident. Claire tripped on a loose brick as the five of us exited the front entrance one afternoon when the rain had let up briefly. I reached out to steady her, and my hand was thrust away from her shoulder. I tried again, but once more my hand was pushed forcefully from her. I shook my head, muttered, "Well I will be damned."

"What?" Claire asked me again, "What did you say?"

"Nothing," I lied.

"You said something foul, John. I heard you."

"I apologize, Claire. I am sorry if I offended you."

"Well, you did."

I blushed, and apologized again.

Claire relented, said that she accepted my apology. I was relieved.

I noticed that Mary was puzzled by Claire's reaction, by her friend's statement that she was indeed offended by my language.

Later, in my bedroom, I mused, *So much for blood lust.* I thought about needing to drink from George. For some reason, I felt disgust at the image of biting his neck, of taking in his odd tasting blood. A small inner voice, a voice I did not recognize as my own, asked, *What about Mary or Percy?* And then, *What about the bellboy? The bellboy!* But the idea of taking advantage of Mary or Percy frightened me. *What have I become?* I thought. Then, I felt disgust at the image of taking blood from a servant. I would have to make do with dead animals. *I must rescue Mungo from the cage.*

✝

Once more, I discovered quite by accident a physical strength of which I had been unaware. While fiddling with the padlock on Mungo's cage late that same night, I broke the metal mechanism into several pieces so that the cage swung open and the Mandrill looked at me with that same expectation he had had before. *Mungo,* I thought, *you must come to my bedroom and remain very quiet there, sometimes for days at a time.* And I swear the animal nodded then, in the falling rain, followed me into the villa, and into my small bedroom. He hunkered down in the corner and promptly fell asleep.

Early in the morning before the sunrise was barely appreciated in the eastern sky behind the steady rainfall, I sent Mungo into the forest to capture at least two rabbits, preferably alive. Mungo proved to be even a better hunter than I expected, returning with two small brown, wet bunnies, both alive and kicking against his massive chest. Mungo banged them both on the hard floor of my room, knocking them unconscious.

Thank you, Mungo, I thought, petting the beast on its large and colorful head. Then, I picked up the first rabbit, plunged my teeth through its soaked fur, into its neck, and drained its blood in no time at all. The second required even less time. I remained hungry, but *at least I am not starving for blood. And, Mary and Percy are safe.* I also could rest easy that for now I would not need to bite the horrid Lord Byron. Claire, of course, appeared to be off limits as long as she wore the crucifix about her neck. I was both happy and unhappy about this situation for Claire's blood remained the most attractive.

Chapter Six: Hospital

We continued to tell our tales, competing with one another, working to prove our story was the best of the lot. My short story, *The Vampyre* which I would publish(ed) later in 1819 told of a young man, an orphan named Aubrey, and of a Lord called Ruthven, a man who was "entirely absorbed in himself." I was certain that Mary, Claire, Percy, and especially George knew to whom I was referring as I told parts of my tale, yet to be fully composed. George rolled his eyes several times while listening to me describe Lord Ruthven. I ignored my former friend.

I must admit that Mary's story would turn out to be the best, a true masterpiece. Every time Mary Godwin spoke, telling us of the mad doctor, I imagined she was speaking of me. I know she was not, but like George projecting himself onto Lord Ruthven, I projected myself onto Doctor Frankenstein. True, I was not no longer robbing graves, any longer for I had indeed robbed graves as a medical student in order to study the anatomy of the human body. Nor was I sewing body parts together to make a new man. But I was thoroughly involved in death.

While listening to Mary's story and marveling at the animated way she told it, I felt that I also was akin to the monster which Frankenstein brought to life through the electric current in lightning. Yet unlike the doctor's monster, I was not deranged. Nevertheless, I was not in complete control of my primal urge to consume blood, especially human blood, especially Claire's blood. I was mercilessly chained to this blood lust. I had been incapable of escaping this need, this desire that was not only physical but psychological. And this deep lust reminded me of Godwin's monster, a clumsy pathetic human animal, otherwise known to me at least as *a kind of living dead. Was I also a living dead thing?* I was not certain I even knew what that meant. Even though I suspected I was an immortal being, I had no evidence that I was unable to die. In fact, several times during this horrible summer, I had felt close to death.

About this time in our dreadful stay at Villa Diodati, Boomer began to bark at me, his hair rising off his back at my approach. Mary and Claire were the first to notice. Mary commented on the dog's strange behavior the second time it appeared ready to attack me, as if defending territory or the personage of its owner. However, George was inside the villa. "That's so odd. I thought Boomer liked you, John."

Claire laughed, "I thought Boomer liked *everyone!*"

"Maybe you are a werewolf, John," suggested Mary, teasing me of course. "Supposedly, werewolves are common around these parts."

I blushed, and decided not to say anything in response to Mary's lighthearted suggestion. She was so close to the truth, I was frightened, nay threatened.

Claire touched her neck, then fondled the crucifix. She turned pale, and whispered, "Maybe you *are* a vampyre, John, like in your story."

I looked Claire directly in her beautiful eyes, and said, "Maybe I am." Then, I turned and walked away from Boomer, the dog that was still barking, then growling at me, its hair standing straight up and as stiff as any dog's hair I had ever witnessed.

From behind, I heard Mary laughing with Claire, "Oh, that is riotous, Claire, just riotous." And I heard Claire whisper harshly, "I am most serious, Mary."

If I kill Boomer, I thought, everyone will suspect that I am not as I appear.

Luckily for me, Boomer despite the steady rainfall suddenly started to run after the silly noisy peacock. When I was out of sight and smell, the dog continued to behave bizarrely, chasing the large bird, pulling out feathers with its teeth whenever it could reach the peacock's tail. Lord Byron was at his wit's end within a few days of this for I decided that I must avoid Boomer at all costs. Whenever I strolled outside which I did despite the rainfall, I made certain the dog was not in the expansive yard and gardens. If I spotted Boomer, I turned to retreat into the villa. Now that Mungo was hunting for me, I had little reason to go outside in the first place.

A week after Boomer began to chase the peacock, George decided that it was either get rid of the dog or get rid of the peacock. For George, this proved a difficult decision at least on the surface for the man pretended to love his animals even though he generally neglected them.

Twelve years prior, when George was still in grammar school, his parents had selected a healthy retriever puppy from a decent sized litter with an excellent pedigree. They gave the virtually perfect puppy to George for his sixteenth birthday. At first, the boy and his dog were inseparable, but when George left for Trinity College the dog was left behind with the Byrons. Boomer only rejoined the man when he and I began the Grand Tour. Therefore, Boomer was now an elderly dog and one that Byron did not particularly love, as I saw it.

As for the peacock, Byron had purchased it on the Grand Tour in the same manner that he had bought the Mandrill called Mungo. Since George had never named the bird, I assumed he did not care much for it. So I was rather shocked that he carted Boomer off to a local vet to have the dog put down. I was also relieved because the peacock continued to show no interest in me or anyone else for that matter.

✝

"How could you?" Claire demanded that evening around the fireplace.

"Boomer was an old dog, Claire," responded George. He reached over and put his hand atop hers and patted it. "I am sorry, dear. I know you liked that old dog of mine."

"I did," admitted Claire. Then she leaned her head against George's shoulder and stared at the fire. George petted her hair, then kissed the top of her head just behind a ribbon she wore there. He whispered, "You are my darling." Claire smiled broadly and closed her eyes. She looked utterly at peace.

They are truly in love. And I have bitten both of them. Did I give them my horrid malady as Mungo gave it to me? I had witnessed no evidence of a change in their behaviors. They were the same two people that I had known before my change of nature. Whereas I was something other than or at the very least more than human, these two remained man and woman, soon to be united in matrimony, I imagined. And they would have offspring, and those children would be normal boys and girls. I could only hope I was right. I sighed as I watched the two lovers. *When did this love affair happen?* The relationship had been subtle for most of the summer, but over the past few weeks, George and Claire had begun to spend more and more time together, walking around Lake Geneva under murky, dark skies, carrying large umbrellas. I thought that I must have deliberately ignored the signs of the romance until that evening. Now I found it impossible to miss them. George whispering softly to the young woman, the young woman blushing, preening.

begin

I glanced over to Percy and Mary and figured they would be married by the end of the year. Two loving couples in the throes of romance sat together right there before me, and I was alone. I would always be alone, from this point forward. No one would ever love me, ever comfort me again. My only *friend* was a large, colorfully faced monkey, a Mandrill named Mungo. I felt my eyes water and I pulled out my handkerchief and dabbed at them with my left hand. My right hand and wrist were still firmly bandaged.

Mary remarked, "You should have that arm looked at, John. It worries me."

I nodded, "I will." And thought, *I might as well have the ghastly thing amputated. As it is, I will never be a surgeon anyway. I cannot operate with one good hand.*

But I faced a new dilemma. What doctor would I trust to remove the hand and wrist to mid forearm without asking me what happened and without telling another soul about what he had witnessed? I began to believe I might need to remove my own appendage, but I knew that I would not be able to do so. I cringed as I imagined undertaking a clumsy performance of this operation with my left hand. I looked back at Mary, said, "I will, Mary. I promise."

"Thank you, John," said Mary. "I believe we will all feel better if you take care of yourself."

†

Next morning, I asked George's coachman to take me into Clarens to hospital there and to wait for me. In hospital, I presented myself as a man who had had an injury that failed to heal properly. After a short wait, a nurse, large and imposing, escorted me into an examining room and began to remove the massive gauze dressing. "Goodness," she said under her breath, "how much of this stuff did you use?"

"All of it," I said. *gauze*

She grimaced and continued to remove the bandage from my right hand and wrist. When she saw my hand, she gasped which I had expected, of course. "My, my," she said. "What in the world have you done to yourself, Mister…" Here she looked at her papers and continued, "Excuse me, Doctor Polidori?"

"I was bitten by a monkey," I said, truthfully.

"How long ago?"

"About six weeks, maybe as much as ten weeks now," I said. I could see her thinking that I should be dead. To alleviate her legitimate concern, I added, "I have been taking very good care of the wound, as you can see."

"But your hand is dead, sir."

"Apparently," I agreed. "It needs removing."

"I should say so!" She blushed, then added, "I will get the surgeon at once." The nurse left the room and I debated my situation. I wondered who she might tell. *Will they be curious? Will their curiosity matter?* I could not imagine anyone thinking of anything supernatural, anything evil, not in Switzerland, not near Lake Geneva. The volcano, incessant rain, and absent summer were the only evil things anyone had experienced recently, I figured. I waited as patiently as possible. Finally, the surgeon entered the room without the nurse.

"Good morning, Doctor Polidori. I am Doctor Eric Meier. I understand you have a problem with your hand."

I showed the young man my right arm. The black had crept up beyond my wrist now, so that my forearm appeared to be dying or perhaps already dead. I said softly, "Yes, as you can plainly tell." I could see his confusion for the man before him should be in the grave, not sitting on an examination table in hospital office.

"How?"

"I am a physician. I take care of it daily."

"But," he started.

"Yes," I agreed. "I ought to be dead by this point." I smiled my closed mouth smile, and said, "But, as you can plainly see, I am not. I am most definitely not dead." Then I wondered, *Maybe, in fact, I am dead.*

"Well, sir, whatever you are, we must remove this thing right now."

This thing? Yes, the good surgeon had called my right hand and forearm a thing. A thing that must be removed, thrown away, buried. A thing of no value to me any longer. I discovered and was not surprised that I had begun to weep.

The surgeon apologized with what I was certain was his best bedside manner. "I am sorry, Doctor Polidori, but it must be done."

I whispered, "I am a surgeon."

"Oh dear, oh dear," said the man, fully understanding my tears which continued to flow down my cheeks onto my dress shirt. He offered, "You can teach, you know."

I looked at him. I admit the anger came so suddenly that I did not know what to do with it. My eyes flared, I am sure for the doctor stepped back. I had begun to drool. Perhaps the memory of my first bite, the bite that took Doctor Hollifield's life blood had caused me to salivate. I sucked back the fluid and swallowed hard, then I said, "Let's get on with it, shall we?"

"Yes, indeed, sir." He gestured. "I will require my nurse. Give me a moment." Then he exited the room. I waited. As I sat on the table, I realized that soon my own blood would pour forth from the fresh stump. *Would I react as I had reacted to Mary's spot of fresh blood? Could I control myself if I did?* I began to shake. I took several deep breaths. There was nothing to be done. I would have to take my chances. Doctor Meier would provide some form of sedative hypnotic prior to surgery. I could only hope I would relax enough to sleep. However, when a patient is in severe pain as I would be, sleep proves unlikely.

Doctor Meier and the same imposing nurse entered the room. "Oh," the surgeon remarked, "I forgot to ask you to change into a gown, Doctor Polidori."

"Call me John," I said.

The surgeon stared at me. He shook his head. "Please, change into this gown. We will return momentarily," and they exited again.

As I stood to remove my suit and white starched shirt as well as my black slacks, shoes, spats, and stockings, I began to shake uncontrollably again. I was afraid both of the surgery and of myself. I managed to get out of my clothing and into the flimsy gown, leaving it open at the back. I sat down on the table and waited, this time for a lengthy period. Finally, the door opened after a brief knock and the two professionals entered.

"Ready?"

"As I ever will be," I responded.

The nurse mixed a fine white powder into a glass of warm water and instructed me to drink it all. I did. The bitter taste left me thirsty for more water. I waited, slowly growing calm, even a bit sleepy. I tried to relax as the woman asked me to stretch out on the table. "Just put your head here on this pillow. Try to go to sleep, Doctor Polidori."

"John," I said.

She smiled.

I spotted the instrument that Doctor Meier had prepared, a short metal saw with sharp jagged teeth and a curved wooden handle. I sighed. I would never use such an instrument again. And, I had only used one on a cadaver, never on a living human being. I shut my eyes and tried to breathe deeper than usual.

The nurse asked, "How are you feeling?"

"Tired," I said.

"Go to sleep now, John."

I smiled, showing my teeth, retracted, inadvertently. The nurse did not seem to notice. Neither did the surgeon who was washing his hands in a basin set on a stand near the far wall. I noticed the mirror. The doctor turned to study his patient as I tried to relax. He asked his nurse, "Do you think he will sleep?"

"Dear me, I do hope so," the nurse said as she placed a short wooden stake between my teeth and instructed me to "bite down hard."

✝

I awoke a few hours later. I was still stretched out on the examination and operating table. The light from the overhead gas lamp was bright. I realized that I was strapped to the metal table so that I could not move freely. I glanced down. My right arm was as bandaged as it had always been since Mungo bit my index finger, but the appendage was considerably shorter than it had been. The surgery had been successful and I sighed with relief. I was alive, and I apparently had not killed anyone!

Chapter Seven: Monster

After my surgery, stump wrapping began according to the instructions of Doctor Meier. Mary was especially helpful, not fearful of compressing the end of my forearm into a shape which later might accommodate some sort of metal hook or wooden claw set in a leather sleeve. I doubted that I would want either of these. I thought I would prefer an empty shirt sleeve pinned up toward my elbow rather than a hideous manmade hook or claw. I imagined pirates with peg legs, and shuddered.

Claire had tried to help but as before whenever she attempted to touch my arm, my arm as if it had a mind of its own pulled away in a most bizarre manner. Claire only looked at me with a puzzled expression and I merely shrugged my shoulder as if I too was bewildered. I could not very well suggest she remove her crucifix. The dying man hanging on the silver cross seemed to lift his eyes to bore a hole in my heart every time Claire came near to me. I wanted to curl into a fetal position and disintegrate.

Post surgical pain management was almost nil. Doctor Meier had prescribed a tablespoon of Laudanum several times a day, a concoction which I suspected to be highly addictive. I avoided it as much as possible. Even though I was no longer fully human in the strictest sense, I still experienced some physical pain.

Mungo continued to hunt at night, providing me with live creatures, mostly rabbits and field mice with an occasional newborn fawn. Fawns were the best, tasting the closest to Claire's blood which I missed dearly.

One problem I had was how to better dispose of the limp bodies emptied of their blood. I noticed one morning that my room stank faintly of rot despite Mungo carrying off the animals after my feasting. I realized this situation could not continue or I would be found out. I had refused housekeeping services since Mungo began to stay with me in my bedroom, and this caused a stir among the limited staff of Villa Diodati. I overheard the bellboy whispering about me to one of the kitchen staff one morning in late July before lunch.

"He never changes his sheets," said the boy. He pressed, "I heard his hand was hideous looking before hospital cut it off."

The cook who was an elderly woman and hard of hearing nodded, but said nothing.

At lunch that day, Lord Byron mentioned that he had not seen his Mandrill in ages. He asked no one in particular, "Where the devil could Mungo be?"

"Maybe he ran off," I casually suggested.

"I still wonder how he escaped his cage," mused George, shaking his head. "The lock was broken. I do not believe even that Mandrill had the strength to accomplish that!" He looked at me, continued to protest, "At any rate, you are most mistaken, Polly Dolly. Mungo would not run away. He is much too fond of me to run off."

Fond of you? I thought. *Mungo is my servant, practically my slave.*

At that very moment, thunder boomed, shaking the villa, and then a streak of lightning flashed straight to the grounds outside the main window. Rain that had been steady became torrential, pouring off the roof edges. The day would be even gloomier than usual. We all sighed virtually at the same second.

"Time for a story," said Percy.

I nodded, and offered to tell the group more about Lord Ruthven and Aubrey. Claire did not seem interested. Neither did Lord Byron, but Mary and Percy agreed they would like to hear more of my story, *The Vampyre*. So, I began to tell them what I had written most recently. I did not read the contents, but gave the group an idea of what was happening in the tale. I said, "Lord Ruthven and Aubrey are in Rome, but Ruthven spends much of his daytime with a countess while Aubrey goes about the city looking for memorials to study. However, Aubrey receives letters from his guardians in England warning him to abandon Ruthven because of an 'evil power resident in his companion.' Apparently, according to the guardians, Lord Ruthven has a 'character that is dreadfully vicious' and has 'irresistible powers of seduction.' Aubrey wisely decides to leave."

Lord Byron interrupted me, asked, "Whatever for? Just because a bunch of guardians in England badmouth a Lord? How silly."

I nodded, said, "Perhaps."

"Let him finish, George," said Claire who I was certain was George's lover. I suspected that George and Claire were now sharing George's suite and his large luxurious bed. I imagined seeping as a mist under the door jamb again, sliding up into the bed between them, biting one and then the other. The image was too much. I grew faint, and apologized to my audience. "I think I had better stop my story here. I do not feel well."

"Is it your hand, old chap?" Percy asked.

"No," I said, "the stump is rather well healed."

"Polly Dolly is just faint of heart," said Byron. "He always has been a weak willed man."

"Do not be mean, George," said Mary.

Claire looked hurt. She was unable to accept that George could be mean to a friend. She did not understand how Lord Byron and I were no longer close as we had been when we began the Grand Tour. She looked at me, asked, "Where does your Aubrey go?"

"To Greece," I said.

"To seek out more memorials?"

"Why not?" I said.

George commented, "I prefer Mary's story."

Without hesitation, I said, "So do I."

"Well," offered Percy, "let us hear more of Mary's monster."

And so, we sat around the fireplace that whole afternoon as Mary continued to tell us about Doctor Frankenstein's monster. Her tale was delightfully tragic and we all applauded at various points. An hour before our scheduled supper time, Mary was weary of talking and excused herself. Claire accompanied her friend and stepsister, explaining that she thought a quiet rest would do them both good.

So, we three men were left to ourselves. Not one of us spoke. George sipped a brandy while Percy smoked a cigar. I closed my eyes and dreamed of Claire's blood in my mouth.

✝

Two days later, Claire and George announced they were leaving the villa. George bemoaned the loss of his dog, Boomer and his Mandrill, Mungo. "I suppose I will have to make do with that silly peacock until I can replace my other animal friends."

"Where will you go?" Mary asked.

"To England, of course," said Byron.

I stood up from the sofa, said, "I will be heading to Papal Italy."

Mary raised her eyebrows, asked, "Rome?"

"Yes, Rome," I said.

"Are you going to research your story?" Percy asked.

"Why not?" I mused.

Percy and Mary looked at each other. Percy ventured, "Well, I suppose Mary and I will pack up and depart to our house as well." He hesitated. "This has been an interesting summer if it can even be called summer."

"To say the least, it has been odd," Claire added. She touched the crucifix and I stepped back from her. She moved to give me an embrace, but we both felt the resistance in the air between our bodies. She moved on to give Mary a long hug. She said, "I will miss you so much, dearest friend."

"I will miss you," said Mary, tears forming in her eyes.

"This is touching," said George.

I glared at the man I had once liked, shook my head, and turned away. I had packing to do as did everyone else. I would be the last to leave because I would be leaving with George's monkey in tow. No one in our group could see this occur.

Before I exited the living area, Percy asked who had won our contest. We all laughed and agreed that Mary's story was the best. Mary blushed, said out loud, "I won." Without hesitation, she took my left arm in her hand, and whispered, "I think your story, John, has to be second best. Don't you?"

I nodded, smiled without showing my teeth. "Yes, I came in second. Thank you, Mary."

✝

That night, before it was too late, I transformed into a mist, slipped under the door jamb of Lord Byron's suite. Although I wanted Claire, I had accepted that I would have to settle for George. I approached the sleeping man. Claire had turned away from him, and was snoring lightly. Her hair was draped over a bare shoulder and I wanted to touch her so much that I hurt inside. Transforming back into my human form, I reached out fully expecting to be pushed away, perhaps violently. I then noticed that the silver chain was not around her neck. I looked around. The crucifix was carefully laid on the table beside the bed. My heart leapt in my chest. I crawled over Byron and settled in next to Claire. I smelled her blood, deliciously rich like heavy cream or expensive perfume. I literally snuggled as close to the young woman as I could manage without waking her or her lover. With the index finger of my left hand, I traced the faint wound at the spot where it had healed in the skin of her neck. I kissed the scar, then sunk my teeth into her flesh. She stirred, but did not wake. I began to drink slowly, relishing every drop. I felt as if I would never stop. *But, if I do not stop, I may kill her. I cannot kill Claire. I cannot.* I forced myself to remove my incisors from the girl's neck, but I deliberately did not retract them. I rested, studying her. *How can I keep you with me?* And it occurred to me that possibly I could make Claire so weak, so ill that she would not be able to travel with Lord Byron. She would need a physician. And so, I once again bit Claire's neck and drank until her pulse weakened. Then, I stopped, watched her for signs of heart and respiration arrest. She remained alive and I could only hope that in the morning she would still be alive.

I transformed to mist and departed in my usual manner.

†

In the morning, at our last breakfast together, everyone who was present remarked at how much better I appeared at which point, Lord Byron became remarkably distressed, and said, "Claire is very ill."

I felt like Doctor Frankenstein's monster.

Chapter Eight: Disappearance

Immediately I told Lord Byron that I would go to Claire's room to check on her condition and report back. George blushed only slightly as he told us that Claire was not in her suite, but "in mine."

Percy grinned.

"Well, I will go up to see her in your bedroom and let you know what I think."

"Right, Polly Dolly." George flinched, revised his statement. He said with considerable embarrassment, "Thank you, John."

"My pleasure, George." Then, after retrieving my medical bag from my room and commanding Mungo to *stay quiet*, I was almost bounding up the staircase to see my beloved Claire.

I entered the suite without knocking. Claire was propped up on a small mountain of soft pillows, her eyes closed, her breathing shallow and ragged, which alarmed the human physician in me. "Claire," I whispered.

Her eyelids fluttered, but she did not wake. Her skin was utterly white. Her hair appeared brittle, as if the strands might break if touched. Her lips were a light grey. The marks from my teeth were the only things on the young woman's body with notable color. This color was mottled purple and red with black around the edges of the wounds. The presence of black distressed me as I recalled my right hand, how it had been dark, hairy, and dead.

"Claire!" I nearly shouted.

"What?"

"Wake up, Claire."

"I am so tired." And then, she opened her now pale eyes, looked at me, "Is that you, John? Where's George?"

"Yes, Claire. George is down in the dining room with Percy and Mary."

"Why do I feel so poorly, John?"

"That is what I am here to find out," I lied.

"That is right," she said, "you are a doctor, are you not?"

"Yes, I am a physician. I am here to heal you if I can."

Claire reached out for the silver chain and the crucifix. I said, "Let me examine you first, please, dear before you put the cross around your neck."

"Oh, John, I just want to hold it."

"Not yet, dear Claire. Not yet." And although I could not touch the crucifix, Claire agreed to wait to put it on or hold it until I was finished with my physical examination. I then helped her to lean forward and felt relief and pleasure at being able to touch my friend. Additionally I was gratified that my blood lust had been satisfied so that I was able to perform my duties as her doctor.

I opened my medical bag, removed the stethoscope, a new instrument I had obtained during the Grand Tour. Lord Byron and I had stopped in France to see our mutual friend, René Laennec who showed us his most recent invention. René told us that with this invention, I would be able to listen to the lungs and heart without placing my ear to the patient's chest. The device was quite remarkable, and so I had paid a significant amount of money to leave Laennec's practice with a working model of the planned final product. Now, I placed the stethoscope as René had demonstrated, and I listened carefully. Claire's heart rate was slow, but strong. Her breathing was a bit too shallow and I encouraged her to "breathe deeply." She tried to comply, but kept muttering, "I am so tired, John. So tired."

"You may sleep in a moment, dear Claire. Listen now, do you remember anything that happened to you last evening?"

"Last night?" She sighed. "I had a terrible dream."

"What happened in your dream?"

Claire's eyes opened wide and she stared at me. She pointed at me. "You bit me, John. You bit me and I think you drank my blood. Oh John." And I thought she would begin to scream. Instead, Claire began to cry. She whispered, "I wish you would finish what you have started."

I shook my head, feeling even more like the monster in Mary's story. "I cannot, Claire. If I do, you will die."

"Oh John. How could you?"

I told the woman I loved, "You are irresistible, Claire."

The young woman glared at me, enraged. Although her voice was weak, her words were sharp. "How silly you are, John. How very silly, just like George claims. You really are Polly Dolly, are you not?" Her eyes sparkled and she seemed stronger than she should be at this point in her recovery from such massive blood loss.

"What do you mean?"

"You are a silly Polly Dolly and I hate you, John. You hear me? I hate you, Polly Dolly." And then she sobbed. "Please go away now, Polly Dolly." She reached out, grabbed the silver cross, and kissed the figure of the man crucified on it, speaking both the man's name and his designation, and I fell back as if this woman had slapped me as hard as she could. Surprisingly, Claire raised up and lifted herself out of Byron's bed. She stood barefooted on the hardwood floor, at the edge of the rug, and pointed at me. She screeched, "Get thee behind me, Satan!"

Claire's declaration shocked me but seemed to have no other ill effect on me or my condition. Then, in the next moment, I expected Claire to toss the crucifix at me, but instead, she placed the chain over her head so that it rested around her neck. The man, still dying on the cross, looked at me and then, I did cringe, slinking back from Claire and this suffering man like a panicked animal.

Claire started to walk toward me, pushing me further from her. Eventually, I was forced from Byron's suite at which point Claire slammed the door. I waited a moment, trying to decide what to do next, what to tell my fellow travelers downstairs. I thought, *I believe I must flee this place and now before Claire is able to tell George what she suspects has happened to me, and what I have done to her.*

In telling our own occult tales, each of us had read or heard stories of men and even women who had been changed into creatures that drank blood. In fact, my own story was about one such creature. Claire likely would tell her friends what I had become, and they *might* believe her. I could not take the chance.

I quickly decided to go to my room, gather up a few things including the Mandrill, Mungo, and leave the villa. I did just that, walking slowly down the main staircase, avoiding my friends until I reached my room. There I put my wallet deep in the front pocket of my jacket and a few other items in a leather satchel that I could sling over a shoulder, then I commanded Mungo to follow me. "Quietly," I said. But I abandoned the satchel, leaving it on the floor by a wall soon after exiting my room as I realized the safest way to leave the villa and its surrounding grounds was as a mist. I suspected too much energy would be required to transform into mist items other than my clothes and wallet. I told Mungo to move as fast as possible into the forest and wait for me there.

And so, in a matter of moments, Doctor John Polidori disappeared, inadvertently leaving behind his medical bag.

Chapter Nine: Rome

For a little more than fourteen days, I lay low in the forms of either fog or mist, Mungo assisting me with feeding, a necessity for any being, whether supernatural or natural or some combination of both. I had come to believe that I was neither fully human nor fully nonhuman. I surmised that I was not dead. Of this fact, I was now certain. I had spent the summer, such that it was, with friends or former friends, people with whom I talked, walked, drank, and ate. How could I have been anything other than alive? Would they not have noticed a dead man? No, I had come to believe that I was most definitely a living being of some unknown kind, perhaps a novel type of being.

At any rate, once Mary, George, Percy, and a recovering Claire gave up their thorough search for me, they left the villa. Only on one occasion, as they had strolled through the forest, had George sworn to the others that he had spotted the colorful face of his Mandrill, but none of his fellow companions had seen Mungo. And so, finally, they had given up the search, packed, and departed by two carriages.

Left to myself, I returned to human form. Mungo waited in the forest while I returned to the villa to retrieve my satchel and medical bag as well as hire a third carriage to take me to Geneva where my plan was to catch a railway train to Paris, then take another on to Rome. The Mandrill would have to be caged and lashed securely to the top of the train, I was told. Mungo protested with hoots and displays of aggression, but I managed to calm the beast and he was eventually secured.

As I sat in the small passenger coach in the Geneva station waiting for the railway train's departure, I thought, *We are off on our own grand adventure without the incessant worry of Lord Byron demeaning me and without the presence of a young woman whose blood literally makes me drool with lust for it.* Then, I wondered what reality lay ahead, what I would do in Rome other than continue writing *The Vampyre* which Mary had said was the "second best" story in our little contest. My reality had altered drastically over the summer. Mungo's initially small bite on the tip of my index finger, my pointing finger, of my right hand had changed everything. I would never be the same again. As the large team of horses began to pull the railway train, my compartment lurched forward and began to gain some speed, I looked about at my fellow passengers and for just a moment, saw them as *blood bags* rather than people. I realized with no small amount of horror that eventually I would begin to consume people. Mungo would not live forever and small animals would not be abundant in the large city of Rome. I knew that I would not confine myself to the countryside for the rest of my existence, however long or short that might turn out to be. And, I knew in my heart that the blood of squirming rodents and rabbits and even fawns was unsatisfying, to say the least. Claire's blood had spoiled me. I wanted, nay, I needed the blood of a young woman, not a girl. No, I would not stoop so low as to murder a child. But, I needed a young woman's blood and I would have it. *I will have it once I reach Italy.*

The trip was lengthy, so I eventually slept on the train, the sounds of the horse hooves striking the wooden ties and of the wheels going over the metal rails soothed away some of my anxieties. I dreamed, of course, that my right arm and hand were whole again. I then dreamed of Claire, that she rejected Lord Byron so that we married and produced a brood of children, mostly boys. I dreamed I was a normal man with normal desires and ambitions. In the fantasy, I became a famous surgeon, a physician of such skill, of such renown, a doctor to whom patients streamed from all over Europe. And when I woke later, I was so disappointed in myself, I wept. A little woman behind me leaned forward, asked me something in a foreign tongue. With her query, she handed me a dainty, embroidered handkerchief with which to wipe away my unmanly tears. I took it from the old woman out of a sense of politeness and thanked her profusely. She grinned at me, her teeth black and hideous. I turned away, thinking, *Her blood may be old, but it is there for the taking.* I shook my head, disgusted with myself for I was not hungry or thirsty and I was only *feeling mean.*

All my young life, I had never been a mean person. Meanness was a trait I associated with George Gordon Byron, not with myself. Perhaps the nasty Mungo had transmitted more than blood lust to me. Perhaps the monkey was endowed with villainy and had passed it on like an illness seems to pass between personages. Perhaps I had become a mean person. If I could examine myself in a mirror, perhaps I might be able to pinpoint that blackness in myself, and extract it somehow. I shook my head, turned back to the little woman behind me, and returned her handkerchief, unused. I whispered, "Thank you, Merci, Danke." The woman took her handkerchief, and smiled again. She nodded her head several times before I turned away.

The remainder of the long trip was uneventful. I had no luggage except for my satchel and medical bag both of which I carried with me, and of course the monkey which I retrieved in the Paris station. The conductors of the two trains were kind enough to allow the transfer of the cage from the Paris train to the top of the train headed on to Rome, so I did not need to keep up with the animal while I waited. The layover was not unduly long, but of enough time to allow me to walk a little, take in the people milling about. Most appeared well to do, smartly dressed, and gay. My stomach began to ache and I recognized my hunger coming on. I did not know what to do. I knew the toileting facilities provided on the train in the passenger car would be more or less private compared to those in the station. Perhaps I might force a passenger into that separate compartment on the train to Rome, and feast on him or her. Perhaps. I looked around, feeling vulnerable in a way I had not since needing to transform into mist and hide in the forest at the villa those last few weeks. I tamped down my thirst, and attempted to relax. *After all,* I thought, *it is not like I will die.*

✝

The horse drawn railway train finally arrived in Rome. Once released from the cage, Mungo made quite a stir in the station. One woman actually screamed when she saw him on all fours bouncing about as I walked along with my minimal belongings and no luggage, my shorter arm evident under the sleeve of my suit jacket, pinned up to the elbow. The woman glared at me. I tipped my hat with my left hand, smiled my most polite though closed mouth smile, said, "A pet, madam. Only a pet."

The man accompanying her firmly said, "Well, sir, you should have that animal on a collar and leash!"

"Mungo would not appreciate that, sir," I said and moved on. Mungo looked up at me as if to say, *thank you, John.*

I said to him, *I need an animal soon, Mungo.*

The beast nodded, I swear, winked at me, and scurried off, across the railroad tracks and disappeared behind a long brick wall. I continued to walk, alone now. I exited the station and looked for a taxi carriage of which there apparently were few. I waited. Soon, Mungo reappeared, running on three extremities because he carried a dead rat in his left forehand.

Thank you, Mungo. I see you could not keep it alive.

No, John. I am sorry.

No, that is all right, friend. Thank you.

Standing on the curbside, I took the dead rat and bit it quite openly, sucked the contents as rapidly as if drinking a glass of water straight, without stopping. I breathed deeply, then tossed the limp creature into the gutter. A young rather disheveled man standing behind me, perhaps also waiting for a cab, stepped back. He mumbled something to himself, then tapped me on the shoulder to boldly ask me, "Did you just eat a dead rat, sir?"

I turned, smiled, showing my extended and sharp incisors along with a bloody mouth, said, "I did indeed, sir."

The shocked man turned, dropped his satchel at my feet, and ran full out. I wiped my mouth, swallowed hard. Then, I picked up the man's satchel, slung it over my shoulder, and hailed a passing taxi carriage. As the cab came to a stop, I laughed, feeling powerful and, as a result, invulnerable. Because I had consumed only the blood of a single rat, this feeling was momentary, then lost.

✝

I knew several people who resided or maintained offices in Rome, but I was determined to visit one man in particular. I gave the cab driver his address after convincing him that Mungo would not "mess up your rig, dear sir. He is a very well trained monkey. I promise." The cab driver relented and allowed the Mandrill to join me in the carriage. The ride was rough but short. We arrived at the office of my friend and fellow physician, Andrea Vaccà Berlinghieri. Although he was not expecting my arrival, I trusted that I would be greeted warmly. I was not as confident that Andrea would welcome Mungo, however.

I entered the private office of Doctor Berlinghieri after asking Mungo to wait outside. A young woman looked up from a desk and asked me if I had an appointment with the surgeon. I said I did not. "We are friends," I explained.

"But, the doctor is not expecting you?"

"No, he is not."

She rose, said that she would return momentarily, then disappeared through a wooden door framing a pane of glass so warped as to be opaque. A few moments later, Andrea Vaccà appeared in the doorway he had opened. He smiled at me, "Well, hello there, John William!"

"Hello, Andrea Vaccà." And I forced myself not to smile broadly. "I hope you do not mind, but I have come to stay with you a while."

The look of surprise and disbelief on the older surgeon's face was unmistakable. He hesitated, then decided. He said, "Well, of course, for however long you require."

"I appreciate your generosity, Andrea, but I will not be staying with you long."

"Well, that is all right, too," he said, relief evident in his yellowing eyes.

"I have an animal with me."

"A what?"

"A Mandrill to be exact. He belonged to Lord Byron, but wound up coming with me."

"A monkey?" He paused, added, "Lord Byron's monkey?"

"Indeed, a rather colorful monkey." And I chuckled. Andrea Vaccà looked concerned. I continued, "But, Mungo can stay outside. If you have a garden area."

"I do, indeed," said the surgeon.

"Mungo would be perfectly happy to reside in your garden. And he will not harm the flowers or vegetables you might have growing there."

"Well," laughed Andrea Vaccà, "that is a good thing then." He glanced around his front office, asked, "And where is this Mandrill now?"

"Outside, of course."

The surgeon sighed, hesitated, then offered, "Perhaps I may send you ahead to my home as this is not an appropriate location for such an exotic animal as Lord Byron's Mandrill."

"That would be delightful, and much appreciated," I replied.

And so, I was given keys to the outer gate and to the front entrance of the house of Berlinghieri. The young woman was commanded to "fetch Doctor Polidori a cab."

The girl stood at the outer door a moment prior to exiting, turned to ask, "Good sir, will your animal bite?"

I lied, "No, Mungo will not bite."

At that very moment, Doctor Berlinghieri took note of the fact that a portion of my right arm was missing. "Oh dear, John William, what happened?"

"Long story, Andrea Vaccà. Long story."

Chapter Ten: Lion

Young venomous snakes, I have been told, are more dangerous than mature snakes because the babies have not yet learned to withhold a portion of their venom when they strike. Therefore, their victims receive a massive dosage of poison which invariably renders paralysis and eventually death. When I killed Doctor Hollifield, I was like a young venomous snake. I had not learned to control the rush of intake. I had not learned to turn down the level of my lust for blood. Now, I was wiser than I had been when I first felt the thirst, the hunger for what can only be described as life. I felt quite lucky, fortunate that so far I had killed only one human being.

The next person I killed would be that very night. I discovered that a window of the bedroom Andrea Vaccà put me in was easily opened. A sturdy trellis upon which a lovely fragrant vine had grown reached the sill and was easy to climb down. Oddly enough, I found that I preferred to climb down face first which was disconcerting to realize. I was like an animal, like a lizard designed to be nimble and quick. When I reached the ground, I stood upright momentarily then transformed into a thick fog that moved readily into the street beyond the locked gate. I had not eaten or drunk anything nourishing other than human food that I had come to detest. I was, needless to say, ravenous having only had a dead rat's blood on the previous day. I slunk along the street, on the hunt.

As a boy, I never hunted. My father, Gaetano Polidori, was not interested in hunting or fishing. As Gaetano's eldest son, having never fished or hunted, neither of my two younger brothers learned these typical male endeavors either. Therefore, this night was my first experience with the hunt. And my hunt was not akin to a human being's hunt. I was hunting in a manner like a big cat such as a lion or leopard. As I moved down the roadway, I discovered that I *had* transformed without intention into exactly that. I had giant paws on three of my four legs. My right foreleg was shorter and I limped along like any lame beast. I felt my teeth with my tongue which had been lolling out of my mouth. The drool I noted was thick, unpleasant tasting. My permanently extended teeth were longer than ever, sharper as well. I growled and the sound was terrifying even to my ears, which stood straight up off my head. I had a mane, it seemed. I was a male lion on the prowl. I protested, because I had learned on my travels with Lord Byron that *Male lions do not hunt.* But my logical protest did not matter in the least. *This* male lion was hunting, hunting a female human whose blood I would devour.

I smelled her from a great distance, and began my slow, steady approach through the darkness of the moonless, starless night. I worried that as a lion I might tear out the woman's throat rather than take her blood. *I must transform back into myself, right before I strike at her neck.* The huge pads on my three paws kept the woman from hearing my approach. She never saw me, never sensed me until it was much too late. The woman sat on a park bench, fishing about in a large carpetbag for something, perhaps a token or a key. I did not care. Right before I leapt at her, I changed from lion to man. I saw her utter surprise as I came upon her neck. I did not wait to see her age or think whether I should spare or kill her. I just plunged my incisors through her high collar into her flesh, finding the deeper, higher pressure carotid artery without any difficulty, allowing me to rapidly draw her life from her until she was an empty fleshy, clothed bag of bones, sinews, muscles, and internal organs. I had taken every last drop of the woman's blood which was not at all pleasant as Claire's had been. I sighed. Yes, I was satisfied, but not satisfied. As I walked away from the woman's corpse, I moaned, despite feeling as powerful and invulnerable as ever.

✝

The next morning, the "hear ye, hear ye, hear ye" of the paperboy came through the thin glass windows of the Berlinghieri house. The headline read "Woman Found

Desecrated and Exsanguinated" in the paper which Andrea Vaccà had retrieved from his stoop and was now reading aloud. "My God," he said, "how in the world would anyone *do* that?"

"*Why* would anyone do that?" I asked. I thought, *I am not sure I need Mungo any longer. What to do. What to do. I could kill him. I could drink his nasty blood and be finished with that hideous monkey.* The venom in my thoughts was disturbing for a moment as Andrea Vaccà reflected my poison in his still yellowing eyes. I asked, "What?"

"I do not know, John William." The surgeon hesitated, sucked on his teeth, a long-standing habit of his that I recognized, then finished his thought, "For just a few moments there, you appeared to be someone I do not know, someone I would not *want* to know."

I sighed. I said, leaning forward, "This summer past was one of the more difficult for me."

"Oh?"

"Yes," and I leaned in even closer, almost whispered, "George took to calling me Polly Dolly."

"Oh, my dear," said Andrea, genuinely shocked. "What ever for? Why?"

"Out of spite, meanness, I believe."

"And this, John William, has turned you mean as well?"

His question was akin to the slap I had felt when Claire essentially called me Satan and commanded me to get behind her, both punctuated by Claire's kissing of her silver crucifix. Tears formed in my eyes, rolled silently down my face to settle on my stiff shirt collar.

"I am sorry, John William. I did not think before I spoke."

"No," I struggled, "you are right. I have become a mean person. And it is so strange to recognize this hateful attitude in myself."

"Well, my boy," the surgeon said a bit too cheerfully, "you must work on yourself, then."

I smiled, briefly showing my teeth, including my retracted incisors, said, "I suppose so, Andrea. I suppose so."

He stood straight up from his chair and backed up.

"What?"

"There's a touch of blood in your mouth," he said.

"Yes," I replied without hesitation, "my gums bleed, dear Andrea Vaccà."

"Oh." And he exhaled with relief.

"What? You do not think I killed that woman."

"Of course not," he exclaimed. Then, he added logic to his claim. "You could not have gotten out of the main gate last night. It was locked with a second key, a key you do not have."

"Ah." And I chuckled. "I am your prisoner, sir."

"Yes," he smiled, "at nightfall, you are."

✝

In the deep hours of that very night, as the monkey lay curled and sleeping, I killed Mungo with a single blow to his throat, then I drank the dead Mandrill's nasty blood. I chalked my inexplicably wicked behavior to a need for revenge for the loss of my surgical hand.

Earlier that evening, Andrea Vaccà and I had sat in his study in his home talking about surgery and its many tools. During a lull in our conversation, I mentioned how I was intrigued by Mary Wollstonecraft Godwin's story of Doctor Frankenstein and his monster. "You know," I said, "I used to rob the graves in cemeteries in Edinburgh when I was a student there. Funny that it never occurred to me to cut parts of those bodies off, sew them together into a new body, all in an effort to reanimate the dead."

"Reanimation of the dead is certainly a possibility," mused the surgeon, smoking his pipe, unaware of my intense expression.

"You think so, Andrea?" I asked, genuinely curious.

He nodded, deep in thought.

"Do you think it possible to regenerate a missing limb?"

"Salamanders do it," he said simply. Then he looked at my arm. "Oh," he said.

"Yes, it is rather difficult to be what I am now that I do not have use of my dominant hand. I am a surgeon doomed to not perform surgeries."

"That is unfortunate," agreed Andrea Vaccà. "What a shame. A real shame."

What I did not say, what I could not say is that my stump had begun to tingle, to itch as if it was alive and growing. I noticed first the subtle tingle after I had killed and consumed the woman on the park bench. The itch came later the next morning while Andrea and I were talking about the horrific murder. At any rate, hope had sparked in the same manner a dying ember comes back to flame. I was anxious to discover if my theory of regeneration would prove to be truth or fiction.

✝

After Andrea Vaccà left his house to travel into Rome proper to his surgical office, I decided to prowl the area around his estate. I debated how to proceed, as a man, a cat, or perhaps an even smaller animal, perhaps as a tiny rodent like a field mouse. For a second, I imagined having fleas. I chuckled before transforming into what can only be thought of as a cute, even adorable rodent, a chipmunk. As a chipmunk scurrying through the deep, un-mowed grass, I realized quickly that I was in danger from birds. I transformed into myself once no one was nearby. Then I strolled on a clearly marked path through the public park. I wasted a great deal of the day wandering aimlessly about, looking in shop windows, studying women who walked rapidly by me, even moving to the far side of the shared walkway. *They must have some sort of second sense,* I thought. They each seemed to deliberately avoid me.

One woman as she walked by wore a large fashionable gold cross on a lengthy ornate chain so that it hung low on her neck. The force of the large cross was palpable, pushing me away from the woman as she passed at an unusually fast clip. *The power of a god,* I thought, smirking. My own mind protested, *The power of faith in a god.* I nodded, smirked again. *Point taken, John. Point taken.*

I had not thought much about God. Now, as I wandered about the outskirts of Rome, I wondered. *Does God exist? Does he see me? Does he care about me?* For the first time since the initial disgust of myself after killing the good Doctor Hollifield, I felt guilty. *If you exist, God,* I said mostly to myself, *you must stop me. Or, at the very least, punish me. You must.* When God did not answer, I stopped thinking about him, at least for that moment.

Chapter Eleven: Doctoring

The remainder of that afternoon, I sat half-asleep on a park bench nestled in the shade of an oak tree's expansive canopy. The sky above was overcast as it had been all summer and now into the early autumn of southern Europe. Ash from the earlier Tambora Volcanic eruption in Indonesia had not dissipated and continued to obscure and reflect the sunshine causing clouds, rain, and colder weather. In anticipation of the even colder climate of the oncoming winter, I wore a heavily starched and long sleeved white shirt and a light jacket with a pair of loose dark slacks that stopped at my ankles. I had taken off my shoes and stockings, and now was wiggling my toes in the taller, cool grass. Once more, I daydreamed of Claire. I wondered where she was. *Probably wherever Lord Byron is.* I trusted Claire had fully recovered from my bites. I was being too generous with myself. My bites had nearly led to the young girl's death and that before her eighteenth birthday. Self-loathing overcame me again to a point I grew restless. I had to move. I sat forward, bent down to put my stockings and shoes back on, rose, and walked back to the house of Berlinghieri. Only the servants were at home. Doctor Andrea Vaccà was still at his office, said the gatekeeper after welcoming me back onto the estate.

I stopped by the kitchen. The master chef greeted me, asked me if he might provide something for me to eat, or drink. I smiled my usual closed mouth smile, declined the human food I now avoided as much as feasible, and said that "yes, I would very much like something to drink. Perhaps a small brandy?"

The man said, "A brandy it is, sir. Take a seat in the front parlor and I will have the houseboy bring it to you momentarily."

I had not seen a boy in the house, but I nodded and took my leave, finding the parlor and sitting myself in a large overstuffed chair decorated with embroidered blue teapots and teacups. I waited. Soon a young boy who could not have been older than eight or nine years entered the room, carrying a bright silver tray upon which my brandy was balanced rather precariously.

I stood up, reached out, took the brandy from the tray, said, "Here, let me help you."

"Grazie, Signore."

For a few moments, I felt my previous natural human kindness return. I sat comfortably in silence for a very long while, watching a bird through the window as it devised a nest. Feeling like a man intrigued by the processes of Nature, I marveled at the bird's patience and skill as it constructed a place in which to lay and tend its eggs and later its offspring. I watched with fascination as the small bird manipulated twigs with its beak as well as pine needles and odd scraps of paper it must have found in a gutter somewhere nearby. *Later,* I thought, *I must examine this bird's nest.* Yet, I never did take the time to do so.

The front entrance opened, and in strolled Andrea Vaccà Berlinghieri, my host. When he saw me, he skillfully tossed his top hat onto a standing coatrack and came over to sit opposite me, greeting me, "Hello there, John William. How was your day?"

"Peaceful, Andrea Vaccà," I responded. "And yours?"

"Busy as usual," he said. Then he paused, leaned forward, and without thinking asked, "Would you like to come with me to my office, tomorrow? Observe? Perhaps help?"

I brightened immediately, said eagerly, "Oh please, Andrea. I have been itching to work as a physician again. Except for writing my story, my whole summer was wasted."

Andrea Vaccà raised his white bushy eyebrows, mused, "Your story?"

"Oh I forgot I haven't told you. Byron, Mary, Percy, Claire, and I participated in a kind of contest to see which of us could write the best occult story."

"And?"

"Mary won, of course. I told you about her story, *Frankenstein*, didn't I?"

"Yes," he said, "I think you did, yesterday when you first arrived."

"But, yes, indeed, I would very much like to help." I hesitated. "Or, observe if that makes you more comfortable."

"I think observation for the first day or two would be best, don't you?"

I nodded, only a little disappointed.

✝

And so, the next day, overly excited like a child who cannot sleep on Christmas Eve for awaiting the arrival of Saint Nicholas of Myra, I readied myself to accompany Doctor Berlinghieri to his Rome office. *Nothing must get in the way of my practicing medicine*, I thought. *I am meant to be a physician.*

The young woman I had met a few days before welcomed me into the surgical office. She even had an appropriately sized white lab coat which she helped me to put on. I was a tad embarrassed by the long right sleeve, but she happily pinned it up to my elbow without being asked. I thanked her. She smiled at me, and for a moment, I smelled her blood, likely not as deliciously rich as Claire's but definitely younger than the blood I had taken from the woman on the park bench. I sighed, and she looked into my eyes, then quickly looked away. She gestured for me to go on into the inner office where she said, "Doctor Berlinghieri is already scrubbing for the first procedure of his day."

When I entered the inner office, the sanctum of surgical procedures, I saw preserved in large clear jars, a heart, a brain, a lung, a liver, a spleen, and a kidney. Each of them had been removed from either one unhealthy person or from multiple unhealthy persons, so each appeared diseased in some fashion. At that moment, like the previously unseen and unheard rushing water of an oncoming major flood, I remembered that surgery would not be possible for me. I, of course, had forgotten one important, nay, key element of surgery. The presence of blood. Once the body is opened with a scalpel, no amount of wishing keeps blood from issuing forth. I felt my face flush simultaneously with embarrassment and anger. I felt incredibly vulnerable and sought to exit the inner sanctum of Doctor Berlinghieri before he turned from the wash basin in which he was calmly and thoroughly scrubbing his palms, the backs of his hands, and between his fingers with a small bristle brush and a great deal of lye soap. Without turning, he asked, "Are you ready to scrub in, Doctor Polidori?"

I was on my way from the operating room when the good surgeon turned. I had rapidly transformed into mist and managed to slip beneath the glass door, out to the front office, past the young woman sitting at her desk, then under the front entrance of the clinic.

Once outside under a cloud dense sky, I disappeared.

✝

As I trudged alone along a dark roadway far beyond the confines of Rome, I muttered obscenities to and about myself. This is when Doctor Eric Meier's words returned to me. The surgeon in Switzerland who had amputated my right hand and forearm had told me that I might be able to teach. Although his suggestion had angered me at the time, now I considered the wisdom behind his words. *I can teach. No, I cannot teach the practicalities of surgery, but yes, I can teach anatomy, physiology, disease processes, and cures. I can teach.*

Ordinarily, the thought of teaching medicine would not have brought me even remotely close to excitement, and when contrasted with my anticipation of participation in a surgical procedure, my expectations about teaching most definitely paled. Nevertheless, I realized teaching medicine was going to be better than a complete lack of surgery in my day to day life. Additionally, I now required some means of supporting myself now that my own education was officially completed. My parents would expect nothing less than a son capable of supporting himself, especially because I was their eldest child, and also because my father was an exceptionally frugal man.

As I walked, head down, I pondered several universities in Great Britain where I *might* settle down to a life of teaching others to perform the medicine I loved, to engage in the surgeries I had lost to the bite of a monkey.

✝

I turned back determined to retrieve the leather satchel that the gentleman had discarded on the day he witnessed me consuming the blood of a dead rat. The startled man had dropped his bag at my feet before running off in terror, I presumed. Now I walked miles in the dark to reach the house of Berlinghieri just before sunrise. I slipped over the gate as mist, then climbed the trellis, entered through the unlocked window, and located the satchel where I had stashed it, in the bottom drawer of the armoire. I had examined the contents of the gentleman's bag on the same day that I had come to stay with Andrea Vaccà, and had recognized their value even then. Now, holding the satchel close to my chest, I knew that the items carried in this leather bag might prove the key to my obtaining a particular position as a teacher.

To my good fortune, the gentleman who had dropped his satchel was the grandson of one of University of Edinburgh's most famous professors. The identification papers within the bag stated his name to be Alexander Monro. I happened to know that both this man's father and his grandfather, for whom he was named, had been professors of anatomy at Edinburgh. Alexander Monro Tertius or the third was not yet a professor at the university, but I knew he had been assisting his father in the classroom as well as in the laboratory for at least a year, perhaps longer. I knew the next step was for him to obtain a professorship.

I did not particularly look like Doctor Monro, but I was approximately the same height and possessed an equivalent build. I believed I could pass for him, especially if the man himself never returned from Italy. Additionally, his only living relatives were his mother and father. His father had been stricken ill two years prior in 1814 and I understood was not expected to live much longer. And, as far as I was aware, his surviving mother was quite elderly, with poor eyesight and nearly deaf. To my pleasure, I also knew that Alexander the third was not much of a socialite, was not married, and had few to perhaps no friends.

I smiled as I slung the satchel, which now contained both my few belongings as well as Alex's, over my shoulder, took up my medical bag, exited through the bedroom window, climbed down the trellis face first, and walked to the front gate as a man.

"Good morning, Doctor Polidori," said the gatekeeper.

"Good morning," I started, then mentioned that I did not know the man's name.

"Oh, I am Giovanni, sir."

"Giovanni," I said, "would you flag a cab for me, please."

"Certainly, sir." And Giovanni exited the small structure at the front gate, walked down the lane to the roadway. I followed at a distance, carrying only the satchel and medical bag. I joined Giovanni a few moments later as he waved down a passing carriage. He turned, said, "Here you are, sir." Then, he looked surprised, asked, "Are you leaving us, sir?"

"No, Giovanni," I lied. "I will be back before dark."

Giovanni blushed, and confided, "I am glad to hear it, sir. Doctor Berlinghieri needs your help, sir, in his surgery, if I may be so bold."

With significant regret, I climbed into the taxi carriage, looked down at Giovanni, the gatekeeper. I said, "Tell the good surgeon…" I stopped, started over. "Tell the good surgeon that I am very grateful for his friendship. Tell him that for me, would you, Giovanni?"

"Yes," he said, "I will. But you can tell him that yourself, Doctor Polidori. You can, yes?"

"Yes," and I smiled at the gatekeeper as the cab driver pulled away.

✝

As I closed my eyes in an attempt to relax in the carriage, I noticed that my stump had stopped itching. I had not been wrapping it as Doctor Meier had instructed for I had been hoping against all hope that my arm and hand were indeed regenerating. I sat dejected.

At the end of the roadway at which point the carriage would have to be turned to the east or to the west, the cab driver asked me for my destination.

I shook my head, said, "Take me into the city." Then, I gave him the address of Doctor Berlinghieri's office.

The man tipped his cap, and cracked his whip so that the horses startled and began to pull the carriage which turned toward the east and Rome.

While the carriage jostled me, I tried to invent some explanation for my sudden disappearance, but nothing I came up with made much sense. A sudden fear of blood? No. I would never have gotten through medical schooling. Overwhelming nausea? Yes, but that would not explain why I could not help the surgeon once the nausea passed. I had no logical explanation that the good doctor would accept as permanent, other than the fact of the change in my nature which I could not and would not reveal.

I would have to return to Scotland as Alexander Monro Tertius.

Chapter Twelve: Monro

Before I left for Great Britain, I paid the cab driver to wait for me "while I see to an errand." I told the man to park his carriage and perhaps feed his horses while I was gone. Before I walked away, I could tell that the driver wished to ask me where I might be going, but he wisely kept the query to himself. Then, he assured me that he would wait and I assured him that I would pay him handsomely to do so. I then walked toward Doctor Berlinghieri's office where I waited outside as a stationary mist. The time for a midday close of the clinic was near. I waited. Soon, the young woman whose name I did not know, exited the front office doorway and turned toward me. Her feet and ankles glided through me and I swirled with her advance and followed after her. Eventually, she came to a small apartment on the lowest level of a brick and mortar tenement building. She walked down several steps, unlocked a heavy door, and entered a dark foyer. As mist, I slipped inside with her. As soon as she shut the main entrance, I transformed into myself. Of course, the girl startled and I had anticipated that she would scream in fright, so I had already put my left hand over her nose and mouth. She fought me rather valiantly, but my incisors found the carotid artery in her neck, and I drank her dry. As she crumpled to the floor of the tiny foyer, I stepped over her and examined the room in which she had resided. This poor girl had lived in a space no larger than a closet. Her bed was on the floor! Her meager clothing was hung on hooks along the far wall. I looked at her pathetic corpse and actually thought, *You are better off now, dear.* I shuddered at my callousness, shook off my self loathing, then found the woman's wash basin, poured fresh water into it, and thoroughly washed my face and mouth. Then I turned, stepped over the dead thing on the floor, and left.

When I reached the cab, I told the driver to take me to the railway station. He suggested, "I can take you wherever you are going by train, sir, and just as fast, most likely."

"Cheaper?" I asked.

"Very likely, sir." And he grinned.

I had lost the only friend, nay servant I had when I killed Mungo. Perhaps this cabby might be a replacement for the monkey. Perhaps. This would turn out not to be possible as the cab driver expressed when I offered my lifelong friendship. He explained his situation. He had a wife and five children whom he loved dearly. He would not abandon them for any amount of money or friendship. I told him that I understood and respected his decision. Again, for a few moments, I felt like man rather than animal.

In the next moment, however, I reached into Alexander Monro's satchel and pulled out several coins that I thought to be doppia because they were gold with some sort of Papal seal imprinted on them. I handed the cab driver two of these gold coins and smiled my usual smile. He took them, examined them both, and grinned once more. He said, "This will get you to the Mediterranean coast, or if you prefer, the Atlantic."

"I prefer the Atlantic. I am heading to Scotland."

"No, sir," the cab driver offered. "I think you prefer Mediterranean. You can take passage on a single ship all the way to Scotland from the foot of Italia or from Sardinia."

I nodded, and said, "To the foot of Italia."

While we traveled out of Rome proper, I tried to remember the features of the gentleman who dropped the satchel. I tried to conjure up the face of Alexander Monro Tertius.

✝

The journey to Edinburgh was long, tedious, and painful. The ship I took passage on ran into a myriad of grand storms on the Atlantic Ocean and for the first time in my short life, I was utterly seasick, tossing the human foodstuffs I was forced to consume, at least a little of each, over the starboard side rail nearly every day of the seven week voyage. I lost a significant amount of weight while living on the blood of the incredible numbers of rats shipboard. I was totally dissatisfied with my situation but condemned to it. I could not risk biting a crew member or one of the other passengers. So, I devised several traps in which I successfully caught the ugly rodents primarily because there were so many. The sheer numbers of rats made it virtually impossible for at least one not to fall victim to my snares. After catching two or three a day, I would suck out the poor creatures' blood in the wee hours of the mornings before my fellow passengers awoke. In this way, I staved off the hunger, the blood thirst I had come to dread.

On the sea voyage, the sun which was still showing itself infrequently had become more of an issue for me. I needed to avoid stepping into full sunlight as much as possible for my bare skin burned rapidly, even visibly smoking at times, and I was still capable of feeling some physical pain. Having no luggage, I had only the clothes on my back. I decided to use my outer jacket as a sort of umbrella against the sun. The bemused crew stared at me whenever I pulled my suit jacket over my head which was only when the sun was fully shining, still a rare event as I have said.

I was concerned about my weight as we approached the Scottish coastline toward the end of the exceedingly long trip. Alexander Monro Tertius was a heftier man than I was, and now I was much too light to pass for the gentleman. I would need to feed, and as soon as I stepped off the ship. I could hardly contain myself as the crew lowered the sails and prepared to anchor the ship at Leith dock in Edinburgh itself.

I could see the spires of churches as I stepped on the gangplank and exited into a new life, I hoped. I found that I had only sea legs and could barely walk down the ramp. A kind older man behind me grabbed my left arm, said, "Here, dear sir, allow me to be of some assistance."

His blood smelled interesting as if he had eaten only cabbage during the voyage. I had seen him smoking his pipe on deck several times during our mutual travel, but we had not spoken until now primarily because I had avoided close association with human beings and their blood scents so as to keep myself from murdering my fellow travelers. I turned, looked into his deep set, brown eyes and thanked him. I allowed him to help me off the ship, a ship I loathed. He must have felt the same as he said, once we were both on dry ground, "Thank God! That confounded ocean trip is over and done with."

I laughed, the first laugh I had uttered in seven weeks! I turned, stuck out my left arm to shake his hand, and introduced myself, "I am Alex Monro."

"A pleasure to meet you, Mister Monro. I am Sir William Arbuthnot, Lord Provost of the University of Edinburgh. Are you not the son of Alexander Monro Secundus?"

I blushed, fearful the man knew Doctor Monro Secundus personally. But, I was committed, so I nodded my head. "Yes, I am indeed. Do you know my father?"

"No, sir, I have not had the pleasure. I have only been Lord Provost for a year now and your father took ill several years ago, I believe."

We were standing on the dock and a sudden and awkward silence followed. I dared not ask him if he knew me, Doctor Monro Tertius. I replied, "Yes, Father took ill in 1814. He has not been himself since."

"Yes," and the Provost cleared his throat, "I am sorry to hear this."

"Thank you," I said. Then, I started to walk hoping that Sir William would not follow after me. But, he did. We walked side by side. I began to look for a taxi carriage. He offered, "We ought to share a cab to the university. I presume you are heading there."

"No," I said, "I thought I would go home first. I have not had a decent wash in ages and as you can see, I have no luggage."

"No luggage?" The man was astounded. "Seven weeks without a change of clothing!"

I chuckled. "You did not notice?"

"Well, now that you mention it, I did wonder."

"You should get your own cab. I am not fit to ride with presently." I leaned toward him, whispered, "I believe I have lice, sir. Maybe fleas."

The man stepped back, then smiled, a generous smile, and nodded. He said, "Then, I will see you later, I hope."

"Later," I said, nodding the affirmative. Then, we parted. As I turned from him, I drooled. I was blood hungry indeed.

✝

I hired a carriage, gave the cab driver Alexander Monro Tertius' address from his identification papers. The driver was less friendly than those I had hired in Rome, so we sat in perfect quiet as the horses clipped along at a steady pace. The driver headed into Old Town which surprised me until I remembered that Monro was not yet a professor, but had been primarily his father's assistant. Now that his father was an invalid, it was probable that Monro was between appointments, without a steady source of income. *Surely the man eventually will have a hefty inheritance,* I thought. I sighed as I realized I might be living in a squalid tenement building. Sure enough, the carriage stopped beside a multiple storied brick and mortar building not unlike the one in which Doctor Berlinghieri's young assistant had lived before I killed her for her blood. I had waited not in vain for the tingling to start in my stump. Now I had been anticipating the itch which had yet to begin and probably would not.

I stepped from the cab, paid the driver with monies taken from Monro's wallet which I knew was in his satchel. The cabby thanked me, the only thing he said to me during the entire trip. I turned, fished the apartment key from the pocket of my slacks, and approached the door. No need to worry about servants. I had been concerned about a butler, a cook, a housemaid since these individuals would know immediately that I was not their employer, Alexander Monro Tertius.

I looked at the key which had a single number imprinted on it. Monro's apartment was No. 8 and on the upper most floor which I knew meant he was a relatively wealthier tenant. I climbed the steep flights of the stairs after entering the front of the building, found the correct door, and quickly unlocked it. I entered a cramped, musty room, dark because the drapes were closed over the single window. A disheveled bed was situated directly in front of me. Books on human anatomy and loose papers were strewn about the floor. Several unwashed plates and cups were set on a low lying wooden table which shocked me. Physicians generally were not known, or at least, not expected to be slobs. I stepped around the books, but stepped on the papers upon which the man's handwriting was clearly visible. Some of the ink was smudged so that the words had become illegible. I picked up one that appeared to be a letter. At the top was a date that I could not make out. The greeting was to the very man who had helped me down the gangplank earlier this day. I chuckled. *So, Alex, you were trying to obtain a position at Edinburgh University, presumably in the medical college from which you and I both graduated.*

That I had ambition to return to my alma mater as a faculty member seemed unduly ironic to me. Surely someone on the faculty or in the administration would recognize me, therefore the transformation of my appearance so that it matched the real Alexander Monro was essential to my plan to take his place. The other aspect over which I worried was that sooner or later, the real Doctor Monro would likely return from Rome. I would need to be prepared for that inevitability. I did fantasize that the gentleman might wind up so impoverished without his satchel that he would never be able to return to Scotland. But this was wishful thinking and could not be relied upon.

I began to straighten up the small apartment. *If I am to live here, it will not remain in such a messy state.* As I stooped to pick up papers and books from the floor with my left hand, I grew faint. My stump had stopped tingling and never had begun to itch. Once again, I was dejected. I had to consume blood, and soon. I pulled back the drapes, looked out at the grey world. Few people were on the dirty, trash cluttered street below. I would need to wait until dark before hunting. I sat down on the bed, leaned back. The bed swayed as if it was on a ship's deck and sleep came readily. I had not realized how exhausted I was from my lengthy sea voyage. I slept well into the night before waking.

In the dark of nighttime, I left Monro's No. 8 apartment, strolled the street on which I now lived, studied the tenement buildings that were in various states of condition, some appearing better kept than others, but all old with moss growing atop their stone roofs.

An elderly man sat in a wicker chair on one small stoop, smoking a long pipe, spitting into the yard, such that it was, now and then. He looked at me, a figure in the darkness, with suspicion. I moved along, not returning his glare. I spotted a stray cat, black, hissing at me. I kept walking down the street, ignoring the aggressive animal. I was weary of the taking of the blood of rats. I needed the blood of a human being, preferably blood of a young woman. I thought of Claire, shook my head, scolded myself since Claire was far from being within my current reach. And, Claire knew what I was! Claire was a dangerous adversary at this point. I knew this to be true despite that I continued to desire her more than I had desired any other human since.

I transformed to fog and blended with a natural fog that was forming across the mix of weeds and grass in the tiny yards in front of the tenement buildings. I turned back to the elderly man who still sat on his little stoop in his wicker chair. I crept up to him, waited, then transformed into myself so that I stood as a man directly in front of his chair. His mouth fell open and the pipe clattered on the stone porch. He gasped, but did not scream. Instead, the old man grunted with an oddly soft voice, "Well I be damned! I be damned!" With only my left arm, I lifted him up by the neck, turned his body slightly as if to examine his head, and sunk my teeth into his carotid artery, sucked until he hung limply from my grip. I tossed his empty corpse behind a ragged row of hedges in front of the tenement building, turned back into fog, and disappeared.

Chapter Thirteen: Provost

The next morning, I awoke refreshed despite sleeping in a strange bed in a strange apartment in Old Town, a section of Edinburgh I had never visited prior to yesterday. Despite having feasted the previous night on an elderly man whose blood was what must be termed *thin*, I was still hungry, or perhaps thirsty. Nevertheless, I felt I would be able to function for several days before requiring another human being's blood. In a worst case scenario, I was certain rats lived around the tenements, rats I could certainly catch as a black cat.

Before I left the apartment, I worked on altering my appearance, not starkly since fortunately, yet somewhat unfortunately, I had met and spoken to Sir William Arbuthnot, the Lord Provost of the University of Edinburgh just the morning before. Likely he would notice any marked changes in my appearance. But, I wanted to begin the process of transforming myself into Alexander Monro Tertius. Without my reflection in a dressing mirror and with only my memory of Monro's face, I was uncertain how successful or unsuccessful my attempt might turn out to be. I would have a better idea when I met with Sir William later that morning.

Therefore, I set out toward the University of Edinburgh, figuring I would need to get out of Old Town in order to flag down a passing carriage taxi. Luckily, I was shielded from the sun by thick cloud cover. *That volcano has done me a huge favor,* I thought. As a result of the heavy ash and the normal clouds, the walk did me good. I was finally able to hail a cab and arrived at the university before the middle of the morning. I did not have an appointment, but I was certain the Lord Provost would be pleased to see me again, and would welcome me into his office for a chat and perhaps a spot of tea. I was not mistaken. The man, once I managed to get past his young male assistant, was quite thrilled to see me again, calling out, "Ah, Doctor Monro, come in. Come in."

Good, he recognizes me as Alex.

Inside his grand office, he did indeed offer me "a spot of tea" and "biscuits. The best biscuits in Edinburgh, if I say so myself," he boasted. We sat in large leather armchairs across from each other and talked about the teaching of anatomy, my father's and grandfather's specialty.

I said, "I am partial to the teaching of physiology and disease processes as well as anatomy."

Sir William pointedly asked me where I had taught since earning my medical degree.

I immediately composed a lie. "I taught several courses in Mumbai."

"Mumbai? Oh, you mean Bombay!" And he chuckled. "I did not realize the Brits were teaching medicine in India."

I cleared my throat, said, "These were several specialty courses for hospital." I sighed, continued, "I was invited."

"Oh, well, that is intriguing," he said, then seemed to ponder possibilities. He looked at me, offered, "We have an open position for teaching anatomy next term."

"Do you indeed?"

"You should be well aware of that," he said, surprised.

"Yes, yes, I am," I said, perhaps too quickly.

Sir William looked at me with a growing suspicion. He abruptly stood, approached me with his arm extended. I reached out with my left hand to accept his offer of a standard, professional handshake. It was then that he seemed to notice that my right arm was significantly shorter than my left. He struggled a moment. I could tell he was trying to decide whether to ask me what had happened.

I stood, volunteered, "An accident took my surgical hand and forearm last summer."

Then, for some odd reason, Sir William asked me a completely inappropriate question. He queried, "An accident with a scalpel?"

My anger flashed, but I kept it to myself although I am certain my displeasure was reflected in my expression. "No," I said and then, in a fit of imagination, I told him how an Indian tiger had mauled me, tearing off my right hand and damaging the nerves in the distal part of my arm. "They had to amputate or I might have died."

"My, my," said the Lord Provost. "How is it you came across a tiger?"

"We were offered a safari." I paused, trying desperately to think how I came across a tiger in an Indian jungle outside the city of Mumbai. I laughed softly, then looked at Sir William and said, "The tiger attacked me. That is all that I remember, Lord Provost."

"Of course," he said, "do not strain yourself." He sat back in the chair, gestured for me to sit back down, then explained again that the position would involve teaching only anatomy at the university. "This is an entry level position."

I leaned forward in my chair, hopeful.

Sir William continued, "Because of your longstanding association with the university, we will not require references, of course, but a period of probation will be necessary."

"I understand," I said, quickly.

"If you are willing, we would like to have you start at the beginning of next term."

"I am willing," I said.

Sir William stood again, and once more offered to shake my left hand. I stood to oblige him. I felt grateful for his offer of employment and said so. The Lord Provost remarked, "My pleasure, good sir. My pleasure."

Once more, "for good measure," we shook hands, his right to my left. The agreement was set, not in stone, but in flesh. I would start at the beginning of the next term, teaching anatomy courses to first years. I did not ask what my compensation might be, but I did think that I would move out of Old Town into better housing once the new term started. In the meantime, I would need to survive on whatever monies remained in Monro's satchel and my own meager wallet.

I thanked Sir William Arbuthnot again and took my leave after sipping from the cup of tea he had offered me and taking a bite of the terrible biscuit.

✝

The new term was a month and a half away, so I wrote to my father in London telling him of my new situation and also asking for money, something I had only done once, just prior to the Grand Tour, since earning my medical degree. I lied to him as well, informing him that I had met Doctor Alexander Monro while traveling in Rome. Doctor Monro and I had "become fast friends" and so he had offered me a room to rent in Edinburgh. My father wrote back with a check enclosed for which I was immensely grateful. He also expressed surprise that I was residing in Old Town. I wrote my father again, lying once more. I explained that Monro's residence in Old Town was temporary while his existing house was being renovated. My father did not reply so I was uncertain that he accepted my explanation. At any rate, I had in my possession enough money to live in relative comfort until the start of the new term at Edinburgh University.

During the month and a half, I planned to gradually transform my appearance to that of Alexander Monro in that I was certain faculty and perhaps some students would not recognize me,

Doctor John Polidori, as the good professor. Luckily, Alexander was only two years older than myself, so I expected the transformation to go smoothly. If I could become mist or lion, cat or chipmunk, surely I could become another human being.

Chapter Fourteen: Soho

Bored with my Old Town surroundings, I decided to go home to Soho in London to visit, nay to live for a while with my parents. My craving for blood had begun to weigh on my eternal soul and as a result I had grown rather maudlin as a man and somewhat lazy as a vampyre. I had taken to transforming into a large black cat so as to catch mice from which I took blood, blood I found gross, and most dissatisfying. I was genuinely attempting to avoid killing human beings, but knew my better human nature would lose this battle with the vampyre in me. The fiend I had become was proving to be stronger than the man I had been. And so, I wrote to my father again, commending myself to my mother and asking them if I might come home. He wrote back saying that of course, I could come home.

And so, I locked Alexander Monro's No. 8 apartment, hired a private carriage to take me to the nearest station where I took the next stagecoach bound for London. I arrived five days later. During those five days, I nearly fainted from blood hunger although at one stop at a smaller inn, I did manage, in the form of my black cat, to catch a rabbit for much needed sustenance. When I arrived at my parents' house in Soho, I must have looked a fright for my mother clutched me in her arms like a vice, and wept, saying, "Oh, John, you look half dead. My dear boy, half dead." My father appeared shocked as well, clapped me on the shoulder, and noticed my short right arm. "Dear God, John, what has happened to you?"

Of course, I knew the tiger story would not be believed by either my father, Gaetano or my mother, Anna Maria. I also knew that my comment, "Long story" which I had given to Doctor Andrea Vaccà and then never explained would not be acceptable to my parents. By now, I should have been better prepared for this obvious question given that the missing portion of my right arm was so very apparent to anyone who bothered to notice me.

I hesitated, then asked my mother and father, if I might tell the "tragic tale" later in the day or "perhaps even tomorrow."

"Certainly," offered my mother, but my father appeared cross with me, so I asked again, politely. My father grunted and nodded his head, saying, "Whatever makes you comfortable, son."

After a supper which my father told my mother "was delightful" and which I struggled to eat with signs of fake pleasure, I excused myself and went straightaway to bed. I was exhausted from traveling and from a lack of blood intake.

The next morning, long after breakfast, again which I forced down with pleasantries, I walked a short distance to Soho Bazaar which I had yet to experience. I had heard that there were abundant women in the public bazaar selling all sorts of handmade items in little shops throughout the converted warehouse. And indeed, the numbers of women delighted me. Their blood scents filled the late morning air, and I nearly swooned from hunger and thirst. Without intention, instinctively like the animal I was, I began to hunt. I hunted for the perfect female victim. Somewhere within the small shops, I knew I would find her. She would be young but not too young and she would live alone. She might be a seller but she might as easily be a buyer. After walking around while examining a multitude of embroidered handkerchiefs, handmade ties and ribbons, crocheted stockings and gloves, I spotted her. She was young, perhaps no more than eighteen or nineteen, very short, and wore her long red hair braided and curled into a soft bun at the back of her head. She had green eyes and pale freckled skin. She carried herself well as she examined a pair of gloves that I had moments before picked up and considered purchasing for my mother, Anna Maria.

I stepped forward, "Those are nice, are they not?"

The young woman startled which surprised me. *Why should I elicit fear?* I wondered. Then I recalled the women in Rome avoiding me, walking on the far side of walkways to stay as far from me, a strange man indeed, as possible. I tipped my top hat, stepped back from the young woman, and said, "Excuse me, I did not mean to bother you."

"No bother," she said, smiling slightly. "I just did not notice you there."

"Allow me to introduce myself," I said. "My name is Doctor..." At this point, I emphasized my title. "...John Polidori. My parents, Gaetano and Anna Maria Polidori live just around the corner here in Soho. My father is a Tuscan scholar. You may or may not know of him. And my mother is a governess. At any rate, I am home on an extended visit." And boldly, I asked, "If I may call on you?"

Again, the young woman startled. She stepped away from me, examined me from head to toe. She stared at my short right arm with my sleeve pinned up to my elbow as usual. I saw pity in her expression, something I had not seen before, oddly enough. She said, "Oh, I suppose that would be all right." And she began to rummage about in her handbag so as to produce her calling card which she then handed to me. I could not believe my good fortune and wondered if I had some power of seduction as yet unbeknownst to me. I thought of my own vampyre character, Lord Ruthven who demonstrated this power in my story, and I brightened thinking I might have it as well. Then, I took the young woman's gloved right hand in my left and kissed the back of it. I whispered, "Until later then, Miss...?"

"Please forgive me, John, is it?"

I nodded.

"Please forgive me, John. I am Elizabeth Anne Talbot. You may call me Beth if you like."

"So very nice to make your acquaintance, Miss Talbot."

She grinned broadly showing utterly straight teeth, fluttered her lovely green eyes, and blushed so that for a moment her freckles disappeared into the heavy pink of her skin. I smiled my usual closed mouth smile and said, "Until later? May I call on you this evening, perhaps after supper?"

Beth raised her thin eyebrows, yet nodded, and said, "After supper."

I glanced at her card upon which I found her address. My instincts when I first approached her had told me she lived alone, but I needed to be certain. My concern, of course, was that questioning her about her household would raise an alarm in the young woman unless she was a completely moronic soul. So, I did not ask. I would have to wait and find out later that day whether she resided alone or with her family.

I said my goodbye and as I turned away, I received a whiff of Miss Talbot's blood perfume so that I began to drool uncontrollably. I pulled out my handkerchief and literally stuffed it into my mouth as I hurried from the bazaar.

†

That same afternoon, I took my mother aside, my father being occupied in his private study where he endeavored to teach the Tuscan dialect of the Italian language to two young students, to tell her what had happened to my right hand and forearm. I had devised a story that I believed would be convincing and tragic simultaneously. I related to Anna Maria that I had fallen from a particularly spirited horse of which I had lost control. I had then tumbled into a stone wall along a pathway, and damaged my hand and forearm so thoroughly that a local surgeon recommended amputation before gangrene set in. My poor mother wept, and I decided this was the lie I would tell about the unfortunate loss of my dominant and key extremity, my surgical hand.

She looked at me with sad eyes and I saw again the pity I had seen in Elizabeth Talbot earlier that same day. My mother said, "And so, John, I suppose you will never be a surgeon."

"No, mother, I will not. I will teach instead."

My mother began to weep with grief. I hugged her close to me, and for the first time, smelled her blood scent. I pulled away quickly, massive and uncontrollable fear in my human heart.

"What?"

"Nothing, mother," I lied again. I rose, excusing myself, and walked out the door to my parents' garden. The fresh air, slightly chilly, stole away the blood lust, and I relaxed. I strolled to a rose bush without blooms and smelled the branches. The odor of earth entered my nasal passages and soothed me even more. I looked at the clouded sky and prayed for relief. I wanted release from this curse of the lust for blood. I thought of God once more, and asked him for mercy. I whispered, "Oh gracious, powerful God, please, please, please." *Silence. Of course.* A cold wind ruffled my black hair. I shivered, felt a sudden sharp pain in the center of my chest, and stepped back into the kitchen where my mother still sat at the table.

I had been raised by my parents in the Roman Catholic Church, but had not attended mass since before going to medical school in Edinburgh. Looking at my bereaved mother, I now regretted this lapse in my obligations to my religious belief for I knew that the beast in me would not allow me to enter a cathedral much less receive absolution and then the Eucharist. *I am condemned to Hell,* I thought. *Hell? What sort of place is Hell? What is it like to be forever separated from the love of God?* As I studied my mother's face, I discovered I could not weep with or for her. I felt only self pity at that moment.

I walked past Anna Maria Polidori and climbed the staircase to the room of my childhood. I sat at my desk and thought about Elizabeth Anne Talbot. *Tonight, I will feast.*

✝

But that evening when I knocked on the door of the Talbot residence, a middle aged gentleman answered. He was obviously a manservant for he wore a full tuxedo, white gloves, and an enormously tall top hat. "Good evening, Doctor Polidori. The Talbots are expecting you. Allow me to show you in." Disappointed but polite, I handed the gentleman my outer coat, top hat and gloves, and stepped into the foyer. "Follow me, sir." I followed the man into the parlor where Elizabeth sat in an armchair situated between chairs that held her mother and her father, I presumed.

single black

She stood, came to me, shook my left hand, and said to her parents, "May I present Doctor John Polidori, Mother and Father."

"Good evening, Doctor Polidori," said Mr. Talbot. "I understand you have expressed an interest in courting our daughter, Elizabeth Anne."

I swallowed hard, said, "I have indeed, sir."

Mrs. Talbot smiled politely, then asked me, "Tell us about yourself, Doctor."

The evening progressed from there with a lengthy yet concise explanation of my age, my upbringing in Soho, my parents' occupations, my siblings, my education at Edinburgh University, my medical degree, and selected portions of the Grand Tour and the stay at Villa Diodati. I omitted how I lost my right hand and forearm, my time in Rome, and my sea voyage back to Edinburgh. I ended by telling them that "I am here visiting my parents for a few months at most."

"Where do you plan to go from here?" Mr. Talbot asked.

"University of Edinburgh has hired me to teach anatomy," I said, immediately regretting that I had told them this fact since I would not be teaching as myself but as Alex Monro Tertius.

"Well, well, a professor," said Mrs. Talbot with some glee.

A comfortable silence descended as we sat on the four armchairs looking at one another. Finally, I asked, "So Mister Talbot, may I court your daughter?" The man seemed to be struggling. I was a skilled doctor with a medical degree and a position with a medical college of a major university, but I was a temporary resident of Soho which meant I would be leaving sooner than later. Would I propose to his daughter prior to moving to Edinburgh? He was doubtful. I surmised all this by studying his expressions as they shifted from hope to doubt and back to hope again.

I stood, walked over to Elizabeth, took her gloved right hand in my left and said, "Miss Talbot, perhaps we may keep our relationship casual for now. Perhaps your parents would allow me to visit for afternoon tea tomorrow." I looked at Mr. Talbot and he nodded, smiled slightly.

Elizabeth beamed like a little girl, said, "Oh that would be delightful, John." She looked at her father, pleading with her green eyes.

Mr. Talbot said, "Yes, a casual relationship would be acceptable to Mrs. Talbot and myself, I do believe."

And so, I returned to my parents' home later that evening having not feasted and feeling rather peckish. The hunt had failed me that day and so I would need to prowl that night at the very least for the blood of small animals before sunrise.

Chapter Fifteen: Beth

In the early hours of the next morning before the sun rose in the east, I left my bed, strolled quietly down the staircase, and exited the front door of my parents' Soho house. I did not feel the need to transform to mist or cat or mouse. Instead, I walked down the familiar lanes of my childhood as myself. I was on the hunt again. The night was very dark for the moon was not making an appearance at that time of the early morning and many of the stars were behind wisps of dark cloud. I walked for several hours until I realized I had left Soho and had wound up in a part of Greater London with which I was unfamiliar. In an effort to take a shortcut back to Soho, I entered an alley that I thought I recognized. From the end of this narrow passage between two high brick buildings, I saw an utterly shameless woman in clothing that revealed her bare shoulders and her ankles as she leaned against one of the walls, her knee cocked up so that I could see a garter on her thigh. *A woman of the night*, I thought. *How convenient. How odd.* I could not imagine her clientele being out at this ungodly hour. However, it was closer to sunrise than I realized at the time. She must have been waiting for the first rush of businessmen walking to the Soho Bazaar for early morning tea and crumpets with jam. Perhaps. No matter, she was there *waiting for me*, I thought.

I approached her directly, tipped my hat as gentlemen are apt to do with ladies. She looked at me, put her palm out. Even in the darkness, I could see that it was filthy. I fished in my coat pocket for a coin or two, placed them in her hand. She immediately bit one, then put her palm out again as if to say I had not given her enough money. I placed another coin in her dirty hand. I did not know exactly how much money I had given her and I did not care. It would be mine again soon enough.

I leaned in, kissed her forcefully and she opened her legs in a manner I had not experienced in my young life. I was only twenty and one, and my education had not progressed as rapidly as that of Lord George Byron or of Percy Shelley. I was not a ladies' man, not yet. Here was an opportunity to gain a much needed education, and so I decided to take the whore in more than one way. I allowed her dirty yet nimble fingers to ply open my slacks, and pull me out of my drawers. She placed me skillfully inside her and I began to moan in a way I did not fully comprehend. The intensity of what I felt surprised and delighted me. I moved with her in a rhythm she controlled. She abruptly bit my earlobe, giving the vampyre in me a signal I could not resist. I forced her head back and bit her neck, drawing a little blood at first. For just enough time, with quite deliberate and considerable effort, I forgot that I was a vampyre, that my intention was to feast on this woman. I was only interested in the completion of my education before I killed her. I worried I would inadvertently take too much of the whore's blood before the release I had heard Lord Byron joke about quite frequently. His words rang in my head, "Like that damned volcano, like lava exploding from beneath the earth, raining down, hot on your body like a giant shudder." And so, I pulled my teeth back into my mouth, retracting them fully, then gently kissed the whore again. She tasted of tobacco and cheap alcohol. I did not care. I continue to move with her under her sole direction and finally, the volcano erupted and I was spent.

She laughed, said, "Well dearie, I would guess I was your first."

I whispered, "You would be correct, madam." Then, without giving her a chance to pull down and straighten her skirt, I plunged my teeth into her neck, found her carotid artery, and in a rush drank my fill. She soon died with a look of total surprise in her dead eyes. I took my three coins that she still clutched in her filthy hand, buttoned up my slacks, picked up my hat that had fallen into gravel on the ground of the alley, and moved away. I did not look back as the sun began to show its rays from below the eastern horizon.

As usual, I felt invulnerable all that day and into the next.

✝

Still feeling quite powerful, late that afternoon at half past three, I walked from my parents' home through the Soho Bazaar to the house of the Talbots. The same manservant welcomed me, but before he showed me to the parlor, he remarked that I was "looking quite well, sir." I acknowledged his compliment, and then followed the gentleman as he showed me into the front parlor where afternoon tea was to be served at exactly four o'clock. The formal tea service was carefully laid out on a large and ornate cart that had been wheeled into the room at an earlier time. Under a silver dome, I presumed I would find a selection of scones on a silver platter with butter and jam in small silver containers, tiny silver spoons laid out beside them. A small china bowl contained cubes of white sugar whereas clotted cream was presented in a matching china pitcher. Engraved cloth napkins ringed with silver and gold napkin holders were also arranged on the cart. I sat down in an armchair to wait for my hosts as I realized I had arrived too early.

Elizabeth was the first to enter the parlor. I stood, offered my left hand to her right, guided her to the armchair next to mine. She smiled, said, "Let us sit together on the loveseat."

Loveseat. I chuckled quietly, mostly to myself, then nodded. We moved to the shorter sofa and sat next to each other, Elizabeth moving ever closer to my left thigh before her parents entered the parlor. I was aware of the scent of her blood, but my lust had been satisfied early that very morning in the alley. Therefore, I was able to accept that likely I would not feast on this young woman any time soon.

Mr. Talbot entered the parlor with his wife close behind him. His face revealed his shock at how close his daughter and I were seated to one another. I stood as the girl's parents entered and greeted her father with a hearty "Good afternoon, sir."

"Good afternoon, Doctor Polidori."

"Please call me John, sir."

"Very well, John." He moved toward me, gestured for me to sit back on the shorter sofa. I did so, but deliberately avoided sitting too close to his daughter.

Mr. Talbot picked up a small silver bell, and rang it. Only a moment later, a maid entered to serve the afternoon tea.

As had become my custom when human food was offered, I forced myself to eat at least a little of a scone with even less butter and jam and drink some of the black tea, insisting that I did not take this drink with either cream or sugar.

While we each took dainty bites from the scones and tiny sips of tea, no one spoke. The silence at first was acceptable and we seemed comfortable with each other. But soon, the quiet became quite annoying for me, and I struggled to think of something to ask the young Elizabeth. I was disappointed in myself when I asked her, "Did you purchase that exquisite pair of gloves?"

Elizabeth laughed quietly, shook her head, a single strand of her braided red hair falling free. I so wanted to reach out and put this strand of hair behind her ear, but of course I dared not.

"Perhaps," I tried again, "your father would allow me to take you for a stroll around the green."

Elizabeth looked at her parents expectantly, and said, "Oh, could we go for a walk in the park?"

Mrs. Talbot nodded, but added, "With a chaperone, certainly."

Chaperone. Dear me, I thought, and realized I would not have an opportunity to feast on the young Elizabeth this evening.

✝

By the first weekend of our casual relationship, Elizabeth and I were taking tea every afternoon and by the following Friday we were left alone in the parlor after the maid served us. I held Beth's right hand in my left and briefly leaned in to kiss her on her freckled cheek, whispering close to her ear, "I am quite fond of you, dear Elizabeth Anne."

She smiled, said, "I am quite fond of you, too, John William."

Then, on Saturday, during afternoon tea with Elizabeth and her parents, Mrs. Talbot abruptly asked me if I was Protestant or Catholic.

I hesitated for whatever I said could make or break the relationship with Beth. I cleared my throat. I had seen no statues of Mary, the mother of God in the few parts of their home to which I had been privy. And not one of the family wore a crucifix, something for which I was grateful. But faking Protestantism might prove extremely difficult, one lie I might not be able to sustain. Therefore, I decided to tell the truth. "I was raised Roman Catholic, dear madam."

"We are Calvinists," said Mr. Talbot.

I had no clue what a Calvinist believed, so I nodded.

Beth interjected, "Come to services with us tomorrow morning, John."

Mrs. Talbot rescued me before I could arrive at an appropriate excuse. She said to her daughter, "Oh darling, a Catholic gentleman would probably be very uncomfortable in our worship service."

I was not certain if I should agree, so I remained still and silent.

Mr. Talbot blurted, "I believe Catholics cannot marry Protestants."

"Oh, Father," cried out Beth, and she rose from the sofa and ran from the parlor, again more akin to a child than to a young woman.

I sat, thoroughly embarrassed as were Mr. and Mrs. Talbot.

After a moment, Mr. Talbot asked, "Am I incorrect, Doctor Polidori?"

"No, you are correct, Mister Talbot. Catholics are required to marry Catholics according to the Catechism I learned."

"Well, that is that," said Mr. Talbot, standing up forcefully.

I stood, nodded, said, "Thank you much for your hospitality and generosity. Give Elizabeth Anne my best, and tell her that I am sorry for everything." I hesitated, added, "Not that it will matter, but I am no longer a practicing Catholic."

"So," asked Mrs. Talbot as she rose from her armchair, "what religion *do* you practice?"

At that point, once more, honesty seemed best, so I said, "None, Mrs. Talbot. I practice no religion to speak of."

"Oh my," said the woman, horrified. She said sharply, "Good day then, sir."

The manservant appeared quite unexpectedly, as if on cue, and ushered me from the house of the Talbots.

✝

Beth Talbot explained to me later that she would have none of it, none of me being dismissed or of our potential relationship being dismissed outright. She told me how she secretively had left her home that same evening to follow me to the house of my parents. There she had knocked on our front door until my father answered. We did not have a manservant who answered our door for us, but Beth had not known this so she had stood shocked that the master of the house was before her. "Hello, Mr. Polidori," she said, "I have come to see John. Is he here?"

Beth said that my father indicated that I had just arrived. Then he apologized for what he considered his rudeness, and invited the young woman into our home. He suggested she sit in our drawing room while he fetched me from upstairs.

I came down the stairs to see Elizabeth Anne seated on our sofa, her head in her bare hands. She appeared to be crying, so I strolled over to her and placed my left hand atop her head. I said, "There, there," and wondered if I sounded like a man talking to a pet, perhaps to a small dog. She looked up at me and smiled. She stood and threw her arms around my neck, tiptoed up, and gave me a quick kiss on the lips. Her blood scent was overwhelming, more powerful than I expected. I wanted to bite her then and there, so I pushed her away not as gently as I wished. She looked at me with shock and hurt eyes. I immediately said, "I am so sorry, Elizabeth. I did not mean that. I like you very much." Then I took her small frame in my embrace and kissed her with passion. She staggered back, and giggled when the kiss was finished.

I looked in her green eyes and whispered, "This is not right. Your father will be very upset with us."

"Yes, he will," she said simply, then kissed me again.

And so, our relationship, no longer casual, continued in secret. My parents were unaware that the Talbots did not and would not approve of my courtship of their daughter.

My mother, Anna Maria immediately developed a fondness for Elizabeth Anne. My father thought Beth was somewhat overly juvenile for a young woman of nineteen, but he did not protest when I told him I might be "falling in love." This was another lie. I did not dare love this girl for I planned all along to consume her not all at once but little by little over the few months I would reside in London.

✝

The first time I had an opportunity to extract blood from Beth, we were taking a picnic in the countryside relatively distant from London. I had suggested this outing primarily as a way to get the young woman to myself without prying eyes around us. I had rented a small carriage pulled by two horses that I was able to drive myself with Beth seated beside me. We found a lovely hillside with a large elm tree under which we spread a tablecloth. We sat next to each other while we ate finger sandwiches my mother had made for us. We also had some fresh fruit and tea to drink. I pretended to enjoy our repast while I am certain Beth did not need to pretend.

Unbeknownst to my potential sweetheart, I had put a sleeping powder in her tea so that soon after our picnic, Beth abruptly said she felt "very tired, John." I suggested she stretch out and take a short sleep. She protested, but found she could not keep her focus. Finally, she put her head in my lap and fell asleep. I moved her head and shoulders from my lap, leaned down, kissed her cheeks, hesitated, then drove my incisors into her neck, taking care to strike only her jugular vein. She stirred but a little and did not wake. I drank. Her blood was rich like Claire's, definitely not as delicious but certainly second best. I was delighted, and drank her blood until I scolded myself. I stopped, pulled away from her, and watched her sleep.

Hours later, she woke. I was leaning against the trunk of the elm tree with my eyes closed, maintaining extreme patience. Beth touched my face and I smiled as I usually did. I commented, "My, you slept a long while."

"How long?"

"Hours," I said truthfully.

"I feel weak, John." Then, she was alarmed. "My father! He will want to know where I have been all day!"

"Tell him you were at the bazaar."

"For that many hours?"

I shook my head, said, "I do not know what to tell you, Elizabeth. Perhaps you spent the afternoon with some women friends."

For a moment, she seemed angry. "What women friends are those, John?"

"Well, I do not know," I said. "Do you not have women friends?"

"Not any I would care to spend all afternoon with!"

I laughed. I could not contain myself. She laughed, too. At that point, we packed up and drove the carriage back to Soho.

✝

Our relationship continued like that for most days of the almost two months that I stayed with my parents. I slowly took blood from Elizabeth, and I managed to do so nearly daily while she steadily grew weaker and became so pale that her parents became concerned enough to take her to hospital, especially when they had difficulty waking her one morning. I stayed away the last few weeks I was in England, but did manage to see her in hospital the morning of the day on which I planned to leave Soho for Edinburgh on the noon stagecoach.

I came to the Talbot residence, managed to get past the manservant at the door so that I might explain to the young woman's parents that I had heard their daughter was ill and that I wanted to pay my respects and see if there was any help I might offer. Mr. and Mrs. Talbot were grudgingly gracious and allowed me to say goodbye to Beth.

On my last day in Soho, I slipped into her ward and leaned over her bed. Elizabeth Anne opened her green eyes and I noted that the whites of her eyes were yellow. *Perhaps your liver is failing,* I thought. I suspected that even if her liver was healthy, the rest of her body was not. Therefore, she likely would be dead within days or perhaps weeks at the most. *I have killed you indeed.* I kissed Beth on her freckled forehead, touched her now brittle red hair, and whispered, "Goodbye, dear Elizabeth. Sweet Beth, sleep now, dear one."

A few tears formed in her yellowed eyes as she tried to speak. She desperately struggled but failed to sit up in a vain effort to come as close to me as possible. I could see that she did not understand why she was so ill and why I was leaving her. She clutched my left hand as firmly as she could considering her debilitated state. I pulled away and took my leave. I never looked back.

Chapter Sixteen: Madman

The normally five day return trip to Edinburgh required a sixth day but otherwise was uneventful. The stops at several inns involved sleep, eating human food I loathed, and taking unsatisfying blood from small animals I caught when I was in the form of my large black cat.

When I finally arrived at Alexander Monro Tertius' No. 8 apartment in Old Town, several letters were waiting for me, most addressed to the good Monro and a single one addressed to Doctor John William Polidori. I sat at Monro's desk and used his silver letter opener to unseal the envelope addressed to me. Inside I found an unusually lengthy epistle from my father. He ordinarily wrote considerably shorter letters. The date on the letterhead indicated he had written and posted it on the day I had left Soho. I pressed the unfolded paper flat on the desk with my left hand and began to read.

Dearest John, my beloved son,

With deepest regret, I write to you that Elizabeth Anne Talbot passed from this world this afternoon, not long after your departure on the noon stage. I assure you that she passed into Glory quite peacefully and without undue pain.

I do not fully understand why Mister Talbot felt the need to stop by our home to tell us of their loss, and your loss although he did not seem to know you loved his daughter. Rather, this father appeared unreasonably upset and angry with you. I do not know what you may have done to make the Talbots so against you. Allow me to revise. More accurately, I do not know what they thought you did.

Needless to say, your mother has been crying since Mister Talbot left our home. The gentleman most oddly refused tea which shocked us both, but especially distressed your mother. Mother, as you are aware, loved Beth almost as much as she loves you.

As you surely know, we both were hopeful and overjoyed, looking forward to your engagement and eventual wedding to Beth, and so we grieve, not as deeply as you or her parents, of course, but we grieve nonetheless for we have lost a potential daughter in law.

I am heavily sorry for your loss, son. I know this loss of your love must come as quite a blow during your first days at Edinburgh. I know you now wish that you had not needed to leave Beth while she was so ill.

Your loving father, always.

I sighed, folded my father's letter and placed it back in its envelope. I reached into the desk drawer, pulled out a thin box of stationary. The letterhead most unfortunately read Alexander Monro Tertius with an address I did not recognize. I folded a piece of that stationary and placed it in the left pocket of my jacket, then I put the box back in the drawer, and began to hunt for a blank piece of paper and a matching envelope. I was unable to find either. I leaned back in the hard desk chair and sighed again. *Why do I not feel sad at the death of Elizabeth?* I shook my head, *Oh never mind.*

I turned to the letters addressed to Monro. I opened each one to discover the majority of them were demands for payment. However, one of the letters appeared to be a personal note addressed to the good doctor. I put that one aside, then I laughed out loud over the contents of the others. *Of course, not only barely employed, I am in enormous debt!* I opened each of the four drawers in the desk, rummaged about for the checkbook that must be somewhere in the small apartment. I finally located it. The funds available to Alexander were greater than I had anticipated, so I wrote checks to each of the creditors, briefly considering whether my left handed signature scrawl would be accepted. Then I slowly addressed the envelopes, affixed the stamps, and prepared to post. I did not wish to remain in debt, not even debt that belonged to Monro. Debt was a condition my father had railed against year after year as I was growing up in his household. Up to this very day, we did not purchase items we did not need. We did not employ a chambermaid or manservant or chef, not even a gardener. We were frugal people. John Wesley's quip, *Waste not, want not* came to mind. I smiled, this time able to show my sharp incisors upon which I laid my tongue.

Next, I turned to the personal letter to Doctor Monro which was inordinately short and to the point. The letter informed me that Alexander's father, Alexander Monro Secundus had died. His remains were awaiting "a proper Christian burial." I realized that I had only moments before written a check to a mortuary for the dead man's body to be handled appropriately. I chuckled and tossed the letter in a small trash can by the desk.

I left the apartment to post the letters and purchase blank stationary to use as myself, as John Polidori. Then, I flagged a cab and asked the driver to take me to the address embossed on Monro's stationary. The driver took me to Charlotte Square where lovely Georgian homes lined the cobblestone streets. The cab stopped before a particularly striking house with a lovely garden and recently mowed yard. I thanked and paid the driver as I stepped from the carriage. I turned, "No need for you to wait." The cab driver nodded and flicked his whip so that the two horses began to trot and the heavy carriage jolted forward.

I strolled to the front entrance and used the huge iron knocker to call the butler to the door. When he opened it, I introduced myself as Doctor John Polidori from Rome. After explaining that I had met and befriended Doctor Monro Tertius in Italy, the butler finally allowed me entrance to the grand house.

Immediately after the gentleman shut the door, I leapt at him, tore out his throat, killing him instantly. I had decided as soon as I saw the wealthy homes that I would live in Charlotte Square no matter who lived in the current Monro house. I did not consider the probable consequences of my actions that day. I only acted, quickly and virtually without thought. After I killed the butler, I transformed into the big cat, the male lion, the hunter. I padded through the entire house on three legs, but found only a chef working in the back kitchen. I killed the man in the same manner as I had killed the butler almost before the chef spotted me in the doorway. When he saw me, he screamed virtually like a woman primarily in utter shock at the extraordinary appearance of a lion in the house. Then I transformed back to myself and found a comfortable armchair in which to sit and wait for whoever lived there.

In the very late afternoon, the front door unlocked and I heard a woman exclaim, scream, and then likely faint for there came the sound of a fall, a sturdy thump. I rose, walked into the foyer. The well dressed lady was elderly, presumably the widow of Alexander Monro Secundus, my supposed father who had been ill for more than two years and was now deceased. I pulled the woman from the floor and bit her carotid artery, rapidly taking all her blood. I dropped her back to the floor and turned away. I felt as usual immense power as I began to examine the entire house once again. I did not anticipate anyone to arrive until the morning shifts, at which time I imagined at least one chambermaid and perhaps a gardener would come to work in the house.

At that moment, I thought of the Monro neighbors. *What will they think of the disappearance of Mrs. Monro and of my arrival? A problem to deal with tomorrow,* I decided. The bodies on the first floor of the house would wait until tomorrow as well.

That night, I slept in the old woman's luxurious bedroom under a silk coverlet on cotton sheets. I slept better than I had since my time at Villa Diodati.

Early the next morning not long after sunrise, the back entrance to the house opened. I was waiting for the arrival of household staff in the back kitchen. When I had come down the stairs and into that area, I was surprised that the congealed blood on the floor around the chef did not elicit salivation or hunger in me. I waited.

A middle aged woman with greying hair and dark, almost black eyes entered through the door. She wore a white cap and apron of a housekeeper. First she noticed the crumpled body of the chef, the man whose throat I had torn out, and then she accidentally stepped in the congealed blood surrounding him. She became hysterical until she saw me standing in a dark corner. The poor woman gasped in shock, but I was at her throat so quickly that she did not have a chance to scream or turn to escape. This time, I took advantage, plunged my incisors into her carotid artery, and in a rush drank all her blood. I seemed insatiable, even to myself. The more blood I obtained, the more I wanted.

I stepped away from the dead bodies on the floor and settled back into the dark corner. I waited. No one else came. Eventually, I decided the time had come. *Should I try to dispose of the four bodies or should I ring for the local constable? Was I prepared to be Alexander Monro Tertius to everyone I would meet?* I decided that I was not. I had to rid the house of these four dead things.

The garden was the only place in which to efficiently rid my house of what I began to think of as human vermin. I found a shovel in a shed at the very back of the large property. I dug all day, taking breaks for water only. I had no need of food. The sun broke through once and while it was shining, I took shelter in the house, sitting in the dim parlor, waiting patiently for cloud cover. When the sun receded, I went back to work. By the end of the afternoon, I had four sufficiently large and deep holes in which to place the dead things. I waited until dark before dragging each body out to one of the makeshift graves. I did not like thinking of the holes as graves, but that is what they were. I had to admit that to myself. I had killed four people, not four human vermin. I struggled for a while, condemning myself, then arguing as the vampyre that I was only being true to my nature. For the first time, I told myself *I am a victim.*

When the large holes had been covered over, the yard unfortunately looked like a graveyard. I did not know what to do. The day was over, and I was physically tired. I went back into the house, trudged upstairs, and entered the master bathroom. A tub presented itself. I had not seen a tub since my stay at Villa Diodati and that tub had been for Lord Byron's use only. Here in the Charlotte Square house, I was excited to see that I had exclusive access to a tub. There was also a large metal pail on the tile floor beside it. I picked it up, went back downstairs and into the backyard again where I had seen a hand pump to an underground well. I pumped water into the pail, trudged it back up the stairs, poured it into the tub. I touched the water; it was mildly warm. The bath would be uncomfortable, but not impossible to tolerate. I made three more trips to the hand pump before I had enough water in the tub to make a shallow bath possible. I stripped off my clothes, noticing dried blood on my left sleeve and the front of my shirt collar. I stepped into the cooling water and sat down in the tub. Soap was just within reach as was a hand towel. I scrubbed my entire body, then sat in the tub for a while. *With heated water, this will be delightful. Ah, this is what it is like to be extraordinarily wealthy.* I was not poor by any means, but I had not grown up wealthy like Lord Byron by way of example. Nor like the Monro physicians by way of another.

After a long sleep, I woke the next morning later than usual, dressed myself in a man's clothes I discovered hanging in an armoire, and began my exploration of the large Georgian house. I had seen the foyer, the cozy, well appointed parlor, the hallway, and the back kitchen of the downstairs floor. I had also, of course, seen the master bedroom and its adjoining bathroom with a tub. What I had missed the night before was the dumbwaiter, a mechanical elevator via a pulley system, in the wall by the tub. I realized that Doctor Monro, probably Primus, had constructed a way to transport water from outside, avoiding the trudging up the stairs as I had done. I grinned. I had also not noticed the large fireplace in the bathroom with a stack of cured wood beside it. Additionally, there hung on a horizontal iron rod a huge kettle in which to heat the water for the bath. I smiled again. I realized that I must have been more fatigued than I thought the night before.

While exploring the rest of the upstairs, my stump began to tingle and then to itch violently. I mused, *The more blood I take in, the more likely I am to regenerate my forearm and hand.* I was cautiously optimistic.

✝

The following day, I was expected at the University of Edinburgh for re-orientation to the classroom facilities and the laboratory in which I would be teaching the first year students. I had not been diligent about transforming myself into the appearance of Alexander Monro Tertius. I had found several sketches of the man in the home of his father, and had studied them closely. However, intentionally transforming my body so that specific details were altered while the rest of me remained intact proved to be incredibly difficult, requiring a great deal of energy, which I presumed meant blood. And so, I arrived at the university essentially looking like John Polidori.

Anticipating my timely arrival, Sir William Arbuthnot greeted me as I entered his outer office. He accepted that I was indeed Alexander Monro Tertius. I was relieved. Although the Provost kept indicating that he was "very busy," he nevertheless toured the university grounds with me, which required virtually the entire morning. He showed me everything. At noon, he insisted that I eat with him in the university dining hall "with the students and faculty." I was concerned a faculty member might recognize me as John Polidori, but I dared not offend the Lord Provost.

Sir William, myself, and the other faculty sat at a relatively short table set up on a platform that overlooked five rows of lengthy tables with benches that ran from one end to the other of the large room. On the benches sat virtually identical young men, the uniformed students of the university. Everyone was eating, drinking, talking, and even laughing.

The food before me was nothing less than nauseating. I sipped on water, and stirred the human foodstuff on the plate.

Sir William asked, "Is there anything wrong, Alex?"

"No, sir," I lied. "I am not particularly hungry." I saw his surprise since the two of us had been walking the grounds of the university since eight o'clock, literally for four straight hours without a break.

He chuckled, "You had better eat something, Alex, or this afternoon could be painful."

I obliged the man, taking several bites of tasteless mutton and potatoes. I drank water immediately after swallowing. I realized I would need to soon stick my finger down my throat and vomit if only to relieve a growing sensation of having been poisoned. *Perhaps human blood and human food do not agree in a vampyre's gastrointestinal system.* I laughed out loud, and many of the students took note of this new professor.

After the meal, I quickly excused myself, found an outhouse toilet where I vomited into the disgusting hole cut in the wooden bench provided as a place to sit for defecation and urination. After I vomited, I realized that I had not needed to expel waste from my bowels for a long while. I had only need for urination. *How curious,* I thought.

The afternoon progressed with a tour of my classroom and one of the two laboratories. I recognized both and said so to Sir William. Of course, I knew these places from my time as a student at Edinburgh University whereas Alex primarily knew them from employment with his father, Alexander Monro Secundus.

The work day finally came to a close, and I took a carriage home to my new Charlotte Square house. I had left the house unlocked for I had yet to locate a key. *I will find one tonight,* I determined.

But, when I arrived at my home, I fell straightaway to bed and slept all night.

†

I woke early the following day in preparation for my first day of teaching, but before I left for the university, I sat at Monro's massive oak desk to pen a short letter to my parents.

Dearest Mother and Father,

As I told you in my previous letter, my lodging in Old Town was temporary. I have now moved into the house of my colleague and friend, Doctor Alexander Monro Tertius in Charlotte Square, a quite fashionable part of Edinburgh.

Alexander and I both begin teaching anatomy and physiology today at the university. Please refrain from contacting me there, and send any letters or packages to the following address in care of Doctor Monro.

1 Great Stuart Street, Edinburgh, Scotland

I look forward to your correspondence. As always, your loving son,

John

After posting the letter, I made my way to my designated classroom on the grounds of Edinburgh University where I found a small group of young men waiting for my arrival. I had not realized that I was running behind my time. I did not apologize. Rather I introduced myself to my first year anatomy students. The boys were polite, listened to my lectures attentively, and took notes furiously. At the end of the day, I felt as if my teaching was, if not inspired, at least adequate.

But by the end of the first week, I *almost* regretted having buried the four bodies on the Monro property. Those four human beings that I killed could have made excellent cadavers for the anatomy laboratory in that the university had a shortage of preserved corpses for study. Of course, I would not have been able to explain how I came by these dead bodies, two of them completely drained of blood and the others with their throats torn out, so my regret was brief.

One of the other professors stopped me after the noon meal the following week. He leaned in close to me and said, "You have cleaned up nicely, Monro. You always were in such a state of…" And the man hesitated, looked at me closely, and finished, "… dishevelment." Then he chuckled. "In fact, you hardly look like yourself, old man."

"Lost weight in Italy," I said.

He shook his head, offered, "No, something is different about you." Then he shrugged his broad shoulders and strolled off.

I realized that I did not know the professor's name or even his position. I needed to study the faculty catalogue and learn about my colleagues. *Will not do if I cannot respond to a colleague that I should know by his name.*

I was also concerned about my physical appearance. Every night during those first weeks, I attempted to make myself resemble Alexander Monro Tertius. Each day, I felt as if I was becoming more like the man, at least in appearance, with the notable exception that I dressed better and tended to my hygiene in a way I gathered he had not. I had learned he had a tendency to come to the laboratory when he was his father's assistant unwashed and odiferous. He apparently had rarely combed his ill kept hair or tended to his teeth. *No wonder he had had so few friends.*

I was more sociable than he had been as well. Many times during that first term, I went to pubs after the work day, drank beers with men I hardly knew. I declined supper invitations, however.

Most fortunately, I soon discovered that I could play with my food at the faculty table, pretend to place foodstuff in my mouth, then place the food back on the plate. If I stirred the nasty human muck around enough, no one seemed to notice I was not eating. I also drank strictly water at the university which did not disagree with me. Beer or brandy at the pubs generally did not disagree with my system as well. Most everything else that I had felt force to try at least once made me deathly ill. Vomiting had become the only solution other than total avoidance.

As for blood intake, that proved difficult, nay nearly impossible in Charlotte Square, so at every week's end, I would travel back to Old Town and reoccupy Monro's No. 8 apartment. From that home base, I would go out at night to hunt.

I found it strange indeed to play the part of a man during the work week, then be myself, an animal during the two days of week's end.

On Saturday and Sunday nights, I needed to hunt continuously in order to gain enough sustenance for the upcoming week. Otherwise, I had to fall back on the consumption of the blood of birds, squirrels, rabbits, mice, even rats, blood I abhorred almost as much as I hated human foods.

When hunting at night in Old Town, most often the humans I managed to take down and bite were either ladies of the night or the poverty stricken rabble who had no place to call home. Both usually sported filthy bodies, and I began to be concerned that their blood might be contaminated in some fashion. As a physician, I would have preferred to take blood from cleaner individuals. Yet, I realized I could not be too picky. In reality, the only blood I desired was that of Claire's. Therefore, I settled for the only blood available which currently was on the streets of Old Town. I was, nevertheless encouraged that with fresh blood, my stump tingled and on occasion even itched. However, my blood intake proved to be so sporadic that no growth, no regeneration occurred. I was again disappointed, and somewhat dejected.

To make matters worse, by midterm, I ran into significant difficulty when hunting. People in Old Town had become acutely aware that some darkly insane man was terrorizing the community, killing whores and homeless by draining them of blood. The constables and watchmen had strongly recommended that all people stay off the streets after dark.

Indeed, I was stopped one Saturday night just after sundown by a local watchman walking his designated beat, enforcing the curfew.

"Sir," he said, "you ought not be out here in the dark."

I produced my calling card, one that indicated I lived in the immediate area and explained that I was "walking home."

The watchman only glanced at my card, then studied me, looking me up and down. I was well dressed. Even my nails had been manicured recently and my haircut was fresh. He looked at me with a wariness I did not like. He asked, "Have you not heard? There is a madman about."

"What sort of madman?" I asked.

"He bites people's necks, sir, seems he may drink blood. Maybe part of some dark ritual, sir. I do not know. He be mad, sir."

I chuckled, said, "I would say so."

"Go on home now, sir." And then he grew serious. He leaned toward me, said under his breath, "If I see you about again sir after dark, violating curfew, I will take you in for questioning. You know what that means, sir?"

I shook my head.

He continued, "It means you will not see the light of day for I do not know how long. That is what it means, sir. It means the constable will locked you up. So go on home now and stay off these streets at night."

At that moment, I knew that I would need to find another young woman like Elizabeth Anne Talbot or better yet, like Claire Clairmont.

Chapter Seventeen: Corpses

While I was teaching human anatomy in the laboratory, my students complained to me that they required cadavers to dissect so that they might learn the internal structures of the human body. One young man in particular argued that he found it "impossible to comprehend how organs are positioned in the body in such a way as to function without actually seeing them!" I also had become frustrated by the lack of cadavers, fully agreeing with the students. Therefore, I arranged a kind of committee of selected young men to go into cemeteries in Old Town particularly and exhume any fresh graves they might find. I did, however, highly recommend they peruse the obituaries in the local newspaper or even better take note of any public executions before their *hunt for the dead.*

I had absolutely no difficulty recruiting three students for this committee who happened to be the three most vocal of those that complained about not having cadavers in the first place. I was somewhat surprised that these highly educated, wealthy young men were willing, even eager to become grave robbers until I remembered that when I was a student at Edinburgh, I had been a student grave robber myself and for the same reason.

To avoid my own risk of close exposure to the blood of the dead, I selected one of these young men, the one who had been the most emphatic, to run the dissections in the laboratory. His name was Ross MacDonald and he was merely seventeen years of age. He was a tall, handsome young man who appeared to be of more than above average intelligence. I thought he might be one of the smartest young men I had ever met. I wished that I could invite him to my home in Charlotte Square as I had several times gotten a whiff of his blood scent and had found myself lusting after MacDonald's life essence.

I began to plot. Surely there was an acceptable, even appropriate way to gather students in one's home, not one student, of course, but a group of students. I pondered this problem even in my sleep, dreaming different scenarios that all ran to disaster.

In the meantime, several cadavers arrived at the laboratory. I had instructed the boys, yes, they were indeed boys, to hire men off the street to load the bodies on carts and bring them to the university laboratory after dark. I had taken MacDonald aside and given him a key to the laboratory, then warned, "Pay these men handsomely so they will not squeal like pigs to the watchmen or worse to the constable." And I then also provided the young man with plenty of money, adding, "I trust you, Master MacDonald to use my funds wisely and to guard that key with your life."

"Yes, sir, Professor Monro, sir, I will."

At the time, I took the boy by the sleeve with my left hand, and said, "Call me John."

"John?"

"A nickname I prefer," I lied convincingly I thought.

And MacDonald smiled, and said, "Call me Ross, John."

I felt an immediate connection with the boy, and smiled back. For a moment, I revealed my sharp incisors. Ross MacDonald did not react. I was pleased.

In the weeks that followed that unusual connection, Ross MacDonald guided the other fifteen students in the dissection of the first cadaver, an elderly woman who the committee informed me had died of "natural causes" according to her obituary. I informed the class that "natural causes" meant the woman had probably died of advanced age, that they might find her internal organs in a "state of decay." I talked briefly about what happens to the body over time, even though most medical men did not fully understand the processes behind "growing old."

As I spoke about growing old, I realized that I was not aging. *How curious,* I thought. Not only did I no longer need to consume food or defecate, I no longer needed to worry about aging or about a natural death. For a moment, at a pause in my lecture that concerned my young students, I nearly swooned. I found my footing, and almost smile at the group. "I am all right," I assured them. "I shall drink some water, and that will bring me back around."

The little group of boys laughed. Only Ross looked at me with a puzzled expression. I could almost hear him asking himself, *What manner of man is this?*

✝

The fear in Old Town dissipated as no horrific murders occurred on its dark streets over the rest of my first term at University of Edinburgh. No. 8 in Monro's tenement building remained unoccupied as I stopped moving in at week's end. Rather I remained in Charlotte Square determined to find a young woman to court. Unfortunately I was unable to attend mass or even social events at the local Catholic or Protestant churches and I was not likely to find an appropriate young woman at a pub. Mixed gender card and table games were also only available in places a gentleman should not go, so I was left with strolling aimlessly in the parks or horseback riding in the countryside, although I doubted I would just happen upon a young woman in need of company or help in either of these locations.

So, near the end of the first term and not terribly early on a Saturday of week's end, I hired a small private carriage that I was able to drive myself, hitched up a single horse, and headed out to explore nearby Dean Village and then on to Stockbridge if necessary.

On the short ride, I enjoyed not only the morning cool air but the solitude. And, most fortunately the carriage had a canopy that could be raised to function as protection from weather and for me protection from the unusually abundant sunshine for late May. Almost two years had passed since Mungo had bitten my right index finger and transferred whatever ailment he carried to me. I had heard of vampyre bats that live in the Americas rather than in central Africa. I also knew of Egyptian fruit bats that do indeed inhabit the jungles of central Africa. Since childhood, I had associated bats with mystery, darkness, and evil. Now, I wondered if some malevolent spirit had resided in an Egyptian fruit bat while it waited patiently for a Mandrill or other animal to bite. Once again, I grew fearful that I had transmitted this blood lust to Lord Byron and, most horrible to think, to Claire. I scolded myself as I was apt to do, telling myself to have faith in God, that God would not allow the innocent Claire to be tainted with such evil. I forced myself not to laugh out loud since the Lord had not deemed me worthy of his mercy and protection. I laughed and then I cried.

Where are you God in my horrible situation?

✝

The roadway soon gave way to a rutted and narrow dirt path which slowed my progress as I did not wish to lame my leased horse or damage the carriage. So, I arrived in Dean Village not long after ten o'clock, where I left my horse and carriage tied to a post in front of a shop just opening for business. The merchant greeted me with a cheery, "Good morning, good sir. May I assist you?"

I could not very well respond with "I need a woman to devour," so I shook my head, then began to look at the contents of the store, textiles, foodstuffs, linens, plates, cups, saucers, flatware, and other necessities. When I saw nothing I wanted to buy, I thanked the shopkeeper, asked him if I might leave my rig and horse for a while. He nodded and asked, "How long is a while?"

"No more than an hour, I should think."

He nodded his approval.

I thanked him again, exited, began to walk along the dirt path. *Surely this village has a schoolhouse.* I remembered my promise to myself that I would not kill a child, so I wondered why I had decided to find the school. *For the schoolmistress, of course*, I thought to myself, once again hearing a small voice I did not recognize as my own.

I walked steadily until I heard the laughter and squeals of young children out on a playground. As I rounded a curve in the pathway, I saw the schoolhouse which was a single white building with a chimney and four windows, two on each side I presumed, and one central door. Ten or so children, both boys and girls, were running around a small area with one tall woman attempting to corral them. "Here, here, Jeannie. Stop that."

Jeannie did not stop, but kept running around the schoolmistress as fast as her legs would allow. She finally stopped in exhaustion and threw herself down into the dirt. "I cannot, Miss Ferguson. I cannot." And Jeannie laughed as if someone was tickling her sides.

I approached a few more steps, then when none of the children were looking in my direction, cried out loudly, and promptly fell down in the rutted dirt path. I clutched my left ankle with my left hand.

Jeannie noticed me first, jumping up and running toward me. She appeared to be about ten or perhaps eleven years old. The schoolmistress, Miss Ferguson, tried to catch the girl but missed her.

I waited patiently as I had learned to do so skillfully as the male lion. Soon, Miss Ferguson followed after her student shouting, "Jeannie, Jeannie, be careful, dear."

But Jeannie was already at my side. She sat down in the dirt next to me and whispered, "Are you all right, sir?"

I looked at the girl and admired her open heart, her complete and utter innocence. *I would no more hurt you than I would hurt myself,* I thought. I said, "Yes, I have only twisted my ankle in one of these ridiculous ruts in the road here."

Jeannie giggled, "I know. Are they not delightful?"

"No, dear," I laughed. "Not really."

By then, Miss Ferguson had arrived and was yanking Jeannie to her feet, putting a long index finger nearly into the girl's nose, yelling at her, "What did I say, Jeannie Martha? What will I do with you?" And then, she put Jeannie behind her, and turned to me, the stranger sitting in the dirt. She asked, "Dear me, sir, are you all right?"

"Thank you, Miss," I began, "I think I will be. I have twisted my ankle in one of these ruts as I told your young protege."

"Allow me to help you to your feet, sir."

"How very kind of you," I said, smiling my usual cautious smile, lips closed tightly over my upper teeth.

The schoolmistress appeared to be slightly older than myself, perhaps twenty and three or four. She was remarkably tall for a woman. Her round face was framed by curly blondish hair, and her skin sported freckles like poor Beth's, but her eyes were a bright robin egg blue. Her smile was warm and friendly. Yet, she showed caution as she approached me. "How shall we proceed sir? I do not wish to hurt you or be hurt myself. Shall I pull on your..." She stopped as she noticed my short right arm.

"You may put your right arm under my left and support me. I will do the rest," I offered.

Together we managed to get me out of the dirt. She helped me hobble over to a wooden bench beside the schoolhouse. I sat. "Thank you very much indeed, Miss. Let me introduce myself. I am Doctor Alex Monro the Third of Charlotte Square, Edinburgh. I teach anatomy at University of Edinburgh to first year medical students, almost boys if I am honest." And I softly chuckled.

"A teacher!" Jeannie screeched.

"Yes, many men are teachers, Jeannie," said the tall woman, apparently unimpressed.

I was disappointed, but determined. I cleared my throat, suggested she sit with me on the bench. She protested, saying that she had to keep a close eye on the children, "some of whom are very young."

I said, "I do not mind helping you to keep an eye on them, if that is appropriate."

She looked at me, thought a moment, and sat beside me. Her blood scent hit me at that moment. I knew I would have to have her if not today then in the near future. She said, "My name is Margaret Catherine Ferguson, but everyone who knows me calls me Cate."

"Nice to make your acquaintance, Miss Ferguson." I smiled, tried familiarity, "I mean, Cate. Oddly enough, everyone who knows me well calls me John."

"John? Not Alex?"

I shook my head. "No, when I was very young, I was called John by my mother." I whispered, "I think she had a losing argument with my father who named me Alexander after his own father, my grandfather."

And Cate Ferguson smiled.

We talked primarily about the joys and trials of teaching until she realized that she needed to gather her students and take them back into the schoolhouse. She looked at me, and boldly asked, "Will I see you again, John?"

My heart leapt. I pretended to be considering the possibility of a return to Dean Village. Cate waited and I could see the anxiety building in her soft, round face. Again, I thought perhaps I did indeed have a power of seduction. In a mystery to me, I had felt the power of my seduction with the boy, Ross MacDonald, and of course, no mystery in the least, I had felt it with Beth Talbot. I also remembered that I had essentially commanded Doctor Hollifield into my deadly embrace.

To Miss Ferguson, I smiled slightly, nodded, "Yes, Cate, if you like, I very much want to see you again."

She smiled broadly, her caution evaporating.

Behind the bench, sitting again in the dirt, Jeannie giggled.

✝

The following Saturday afternoon, I rented a slightly larger carriage requiring two horses and traveled the one mile to Dean Village. I had told Cate the day and approximate time that I would come to her village and she had agreed to meet me by the largest of the watermills on the Water of Leith. She told me this watermill was *the* village landmark that I would be able to recognize quite easily.

I drove the carriage past the little schoolhouse and saw a tall wooden building with a large spoked wheel turning in the water beside it, "grinding grains," according to Cate. I stopped the carriage, got down from the seat, and gave each horse a portion of apple that I had purchased at the shop on the edge of Dean Village where I had stopped the week's end before. As the horses ate the apple pieces, I sat on a short brick wall and watched the wheel churning through the water. I sighed, thinking that *the world is lovely.* And then, *I am so tired of this cursed blood lust, so tired.* I tossed the remainder of the apple into the water below me and watched as it was carried away downstream in a rushing foam.

Cate came up behind me, said, "Hello, John."

I had sensed her presence, smelling her blood first then hearing her footfalls on the grass and weeds. I turned, stood, took her right hand in my left and kissed the back of her bare hand. Her blood scent was powerful but I had consumed the blood of five rabbits on the day before so that I might resist killing this woman I had just met. I raised my eyes to her blue ones, said, "Good afternoon, Cate."

Cate blushed when I asked, "Shall we take a ride?" She looked at the fine horses and the shiny black carriage with silver trim, and smiled. "Why yes, John, I would love to take a ride. Where shall we go?"

I wanted to take her to my house in Charlotte Square, but assumed her caution would come back on her and she would grow afraid, so I said, "Is there some place you would like to show me?"

She laughed, said, "Well, there are ten other mills here in Dean Village."

"Ten?"

"Yes, all grinding different kinds of grains."

"All watermills?"

"Yes, all along the Water of Leith."

I looked at the river winding through the deep valley and said, "A lovely river."

"The path is not very easy for horses and a carriage. We might as well walk along the riverbank," said Cate. "You may leave the horses and buggy here. They will be safe. No one in Dean will bother with them. Trust me."

Trust me. How strange that I am expecting this young woman to trust me enough to come to my home in Edinburgh and soon.

I smiled, said, "I trust you, Cate."

"Well, then, let us go along here." And she pointed to a narrow path through a stand of trees, a path I assumed ran parallel to the river below.

Our walk was pleasant enough. Cate showed me each watermill, but I could hardly take my eyes off of her lovely neck. I was grateful that she was not wearing a cross or worse, a crucifix, and could only hope that she never would. I wanted to find out if she attended church services, but knew that if I asked her about her religious practices, she would naturally ask me about mine. My Roman Catholic faith of my childhood that had been bashed and battered over the past two years was not a subject I wished to broach.

Cate cleared her throat, asked, "How is it teaching anatomy?"

I chuckled, said, "I am not a very good instructor, Cate. I even bore myself."

"Oh," she said, "I am sure that is not true."

I shook my head for it *was* true. I was bored and boring during the long hours of my day of teaching. The only part from which I gained even a minuscule of enjoyment was the dissection of the cadavers in the laboratory. Watching the young Ross MacDonald with a scalpel was like inhaling an intoxicating drug, making me heady and lighthearted. I whispered softly not aware that Cate might hear me, "I loved surgery."

"Loved it?"

I looked at her, startled. "Yes," I said, "I have always loved surgery. There is something powerful about cutting open a human body to heal it."

"I can only imagine." She stopped, stooped to pick a small grouping of bluebells from the side of the path. "Are they not lovely?"

"Yes, Cate, like your eyes."

And then, the young schoolmistress did fully blush, her cheeks growing rosy and her eyes glistening. "Oh John. You are sweet."

Inside I screamed *No I am not. Run, Cate. Run.* But I said, "So are you, dear Cate. So are you." And I took her in my arms gently and kissed her forehead, then her right cheek, and then found her lips and kissed her ever so slightly until she responded. Then I kissed her with passion until we were both panting and then laughing together.

Suddenly, Cate said, "I think perhaps we should head back to your horses. I imagine they are getting lonely."

I chuckled again, "Do horses get lonely?"

"Oh of course they do, John. Come on." She pulled on my right shoulder far above my elbow and began to walk back along the narrow, uneven path. While she moved, she asked, "How is your ankle?"

"Obviously healed," I said without hesitation.

"You are a quick healer."

"I am. I am a doctor. Makes all the difference."

"Oh John!" And we laughed again. For a few moments while walking back to my rental carriage and the two lonely horses, holding Cate's hand, I felt like man, not animal.

✝

When Cate and I parted just prior to sunset after talking and talking and kissing once or twice more, I asked her if I might return next week's end to take her into Edinburgh for an evening of perhaps theatre or music. I hesitated and added, "Or drinks." She only looked at me. Then, I cajoled her with "Edinburgh, it is only a mile from here!"

Cate said, "I will see you next week's end, on Saturday?"

"Around sunset?"

"Will you pick me up at my home?"

"Definitely," I said.

"Let me show you where it is," she offered and again, my heart leapt. And then, she and I climbed into the carriage. I flicked the whip gently in the direction of the horses, both of which trotted in unison slowly to her home. There I helped Cate down from the carriage and escorted her to her small porch. I kissed her once more, to say "good evening." Then, I walked away, leaving her standing on her small porch. Cate waved at me, then turned, entered her cottage, and shut her door.

I drove in the steadily darkening evening the one mile to my house in Charlotte Square.

Chapter Eighteen: Ross

During the following week at the laboratory, Ross MacDonald proved to be an excellent assistant for me as an educator. His skill with a scalpel was quite phenomenal considering his young age and lack of experience although he did confide in me that as a boy he had enjoyed cutting open frogs, squirrels, rabbits, and once or twice even kittens. "But never puppies," he added.

"Odd, is it not," I said, "how for many of us, dogs are off limits. We just cannot imagine harming a puppy."

"I could never," was all he said to that.

Ross took charge of my other pupils, helping them with their dissections, then with their sketches of the organs removed from the dead bodies. No one but myself ever called them "corpses" or "dead bodies." All the students called them "cadavers." Of course, technically the students were correct and I was incorrect for "dead bodies" naturally decayed rapidly whereas "cadavers" were preserved with chemicals in the laboratory and decayed more slowly unless kept very cold in ice boxes routinely refreshed which took a lot of man power and ice, neither of which the university could afford.

At any rate, I certainly could be around and even touch a "dead body" but I could not take any chances by cutting into one. Often, I dreamed of being exposed to blood in the laboratory and transforming into a maniacal fiend who killed all my students in a fit of blood lust. I would always wake shuddering and even sobbing. Of course, if the university had been well stocked with better preserved cadavers whose blood and other bodily fluids had had time to "dry out," then my fears of exposure would have been less. Needless to say, decay of cadavers was always going to be a problem, so I remained wisely cautious around my committee's "fresh" corpses.

✝

The term was nearing completion. In anticipation of the upcoming break, I took Ross aside Wednesday morning of that final week to ask him if he might like to work for me as an official teaching assistant during the next full term.

In response to my offer of employment, MacDonald confessed, "Professor Monro, I mean John, I may not be here next term. I am thinking of changing universities."

Shocked and momentarily angry, I asked, "Whatever for?"

"I am thinking of joining the medical college at the University of Glasgow. Glasgow is growing faster than Edinburgh, and I think my prospects after graduating will be much better there." He paused, added, "I believe the time to make connections is now, not later."

I stepped back, glanced around at the empty laboratory, breathed deeply, and imagined tearing out the boy's throat as a male lion, but I resisted the impulse. Instead, I said, "Ross, would you come to my residence so we may discuss this in depth. I can offer you a meager supper with wine and bread, or perhaps tea and scones."

Ross looked surprised.

I said, "Please Ross. I need you to agree to become my assistant. I would like to discuss compensation." Then I added, "Privately, between us."

The young man hesitated, then nodded. "What time, sir?"

"Which do you prefer? Wine and bread or tea and scones?"

"Wine, sir."

"In that case, six o'clock this Friday," I said.

"Yes, sir," he said, then he left the laboratory.

✝

Rather than purchase meat and vegetables for a meager supper that only Ross would enjoy, I instead bought an expensive red wine, Caerphilly, Double Gloucester, and Roquefort cheeses, and rounds of sourdough and leavened breads. I thought I might be able to drink the wine with him while avoiding the cheese and bread.

Ross MacDonald arrived on time. When I opened the front entrance to his knock, I could see that he was surprised that I had no butler. As he entered, I saw concern in his eyes. "My butler is given relief on Friday evenings, Ross," I said to assuage his growing caution.

The young man nodded, and allowed me to usher him into the expansive dining room. The table was immense, but I had set two places of Monro's fine china, silverware, and embroidered napkins at the far end with myself at its head and Ross seated to my left. The wine bottle was open, the cheeses and breads cut and laid out quite handsomely on two large fine china platters. I even remembered to provide crystal glasses of water from my well, and cow's butter from the ice box.

I said, "I decided it was too hot to serve meat and potatoes."

Ross nodded.

"Shall we?"

Again, the boy nodded and slowly step toward the table. He turned and confessed again, "I do not think I will stay at Edinburgh, sir."

"Well, that is what we will talk out," I said, trying to remain cheerful.

"Yes, sir."

We sat and I poured the red wine into our glasses. I raised my glass for a quick toast. Ross lifted his and said, "May I?"

"Certainly," I said.

Ross, holding his wine glass in the air before him, said, "To Professor Alexander Monro Tertius, the best anatomy professor I could have hoped for."

I blushed for I knew I was not the "best anatomy professor."

Ross waited for me to clink my glass against his. When I did not, he sipped the wine which I could see by his expression was exquisite. I took a deep breath and cautiously sipped the wine, scolding myself that I had not tried it earlier in privacy. I tasted it. The wine *was* exquisite primarily because I *could* taste it. Usually, human foodstuffs and drinks were inordinately bland. However, this wine was full bodied and flavorful. I took another small sip. I looked at Ross, said, "Good?"

"Yes, sir, excellent choice."

"Have some cheese and bread," I suggested.

Ross selected one piece of each of the three cheeses and two slices of each bread. He took several bites and alternated the solids with either water or wine, then he asked, "Are you not eating, sir?"

"Please call me John, Ross."

"John," he replied obediently. He glanced at my empty plate.

I offered, "No, I do not usually eat in the evenings."

Ross raised his eyebrows. I could see that he was struggling with some sort of puzzle. He leaned toward me, said, "But John, you do not eat at the university either, not once all day."

Carley Eason Evans   The Vampyre's Witching Hour

I nodded. I could not deny what was obviously true and that this smart young man had observed himself. Ross did not wait for my acknowledgment or denial, but continued, "You do not eat at all, do you, sir?"

"I suggest," I said coldly, "you do not go there, Ross MacDonald." And without intention, instinctively like an animal under threat, I showed the boy my teeth, my incisors fully extended and sharp.

"Holy Mother of God," cried the shocked young man. He stood straight up from his chair, knocking the expensive wine onto the tablecloth. For a moment, I was mesmerized by the spread of the dark wine stain on the white of the cloth. But, in the next moment, I discovered I was atop Ross MacDonald, holding the terrified boy down with a massive paw. I had transformed into the lion, leapt onto the table, knocking over the wine bottle, scattering the cheeses and breads, plates and silverware and napkins, my claws twisting the tablecloth. I now was preparing to tear out his throat. At the last second, I turned back to myself, and plunged my incisors into his jugular vein, having no intention of killing the boy. Instead, I wondered if I might turn this young man, *make him like me but less powerful*. I had no idea if this was possible. I did know that I would keep him prisoner in my house, that I would use him the same way I had used Beth. While I was drinking his blood, Ross was clawing at me, at my face, even pulling my hair. None of this hurt, instead it annoyed. I was thinking all the while, imagining that with Cate Ferguson, I might remain a man, avoiding doing to her what I was now doing to Ross MacDonald. I very much liked this possibility. I continue to drink, but ever so slowly, careful not to murder Ross.

Chapter Nineteen: Cate

Ross MacDonald eventually lost consciousness. I dragged him by his legs into the root cellar that I had discovered on one of many tours I took of the Monro house, exploring closets, nooks and crannies, attic and cellar. I put irons I had recently purchased in the Dean Village shop for just this purpose on Ross' ankles and wrists, and literally chained the boy to a supporting post near the center of the house. I did not want to gag him, fearful he might somehow choke to death. I had already taken more blood from his body than I had intended, but I was grateful that I was satiated. Seeing Cate the next day would be pleasurable for the blood lust would be nil, at least for that day.

But, how to keep MacDonald quiet? I could give him sleeping powders, turning him into a limp, uninteresting blood bag. I did not wish to do this to such an intelligent and handsome young man who now would never be a surgeon. So, I woke him, slapping him hard across the cheek with my left hand until he stirred and opened his eyes. When he regained his focus and realized his condition, he glared at me with anger and terror.

I leaned in close, and backed away immediately for his blood scent was still in my nose and his taste still in my mouth and I wanted more of him. I growled at him, not as lion but as vampyre. I showed him my teeth, still bloody, and licked my still extended incisors with my tongue which even to me seemed longer than normal. I warned, "If you cry out, Ross, I will ravage you again until you become what I am."

I wisely had realized that the threat of death would probably ~~be a threat to~~ relieve the boy of fear and suffering, but the threat of becoming something inhuman would be terrifying. I was correct. He began to shake, and whispered hoarsely as he was quite weakened, "I will be quiet. Please John, do not!"

"It is not my intention to kill or transform you, Ross." I smiled fully. "I need you."

Ross began to cry. He whispered, "I am what you eat."

I nodded and began to weep with the boy.

He looked at me, asked, "Why do *you* weep?"

"Because, dear Ross, I was like you once and so very much wish to be so again."

Ross looked utterly surprised, and closed his eyes perhaps in a vain attempt to pretend vampyres could not exist. I watched him for a few moments until I realized the boy had lost consciousness again. Then I left him chained to the post, trusting his promise to remain quiet.

✝

The next day, as arranged, I rented a smaller, even fancier rig with a single white horse and drove the one mile into Dean Village to Cate Ferguson's small cottage, arriving thirty minutes after I left my home. During that half hour, I had difficulty not thinking about poor Ross in the root cellar. I had forgotten to give him food and water before I left. Given that I never felt hunger for human food, it was difficult for me to conceive of that hunger. *If he dies, I am truly a fool.* Several times, I nearly turned the rig around to return and feed and water my *blood bag.* As a physician, I kept telling myself that I should. *The boy is massively fluid deprived given the amount of blood I took last evening. I should turn around.* But, as a man and vampyre, I wanted to reach Cate as quickly as possible, so I did not turn around. And by the time I arrived at Cate's home, I had convinced myself that Ross would not die.

When I knocked on the door to her house and Cate answered, I could tell that she was overjoyed to see me on her tiny porch. I waited to see if she might invite me into her cozy appearing home. She did not, likely because this behavior might have been viewed by me, a gentleman physician, as too forward for a female. Of course, as a vampyre, that behavior would not have phased me in the least. In fact, as vampyre, I had been hoping for an invitation to enter her cottage.

I took her right hand in my left, and said, "Shall we?"

She nodded and stepped onto the porch. I had purchased two tickets to see William Shakespeare's *Romeo and Juliet* at the Royal Theatre staged by the Drury Lane theatrical company touring out of London. I was looking forward to the evening, including the presumed extraordinary performances by famed actress, Elizabeth O'Neill as Juliet and even more famous actor, John Philip Kemble as Romeo. As a young human male, I had very much loved attending plays. As a vampyre, this would be my first outing to the theatre.

When I told Cate where we were going for our Saturday evening *date*, she was delighted. However, she noted that "I may not be properly dressed" after commenting on my tuxedo and top hat which fit me rather loosely for they had belonged to the real Alexander Monro Tertius. I glanced at her simple linen dress, told her she was beautiful. With that reassurance, we started to Edinburgh in my luxuriously appointed carriage.

Along the way, Ross MacDonald continued to intrude upon my thoughts and sour my mood. I asked Cate, "Would you mind terribly if we stopped by my home in Charlotte Square? You may wait in the carriage and keep the horse from getting lonely while I step in and take care of something I forgot to do in my rush to your side."

She grinned and said, "Of course, John."

✝

Twenty minutes later, I pulled the carriage to the curb of Great Stuart Street, almost jumped down. Instead, I calmed myself, stepped from my seat, and walked steadily to my front entrance. I pretended to speak to someone, an imaginary butler, on the other side of the door, hidden in the foyer. Then I closed the front door, climbed down the stairs into the root cellar. Ross was alive, but moaning.

I walked back upstairs and fetched water from the ice box, a few pieces each of the cheese and breads, and took all back down to the young prisoner. I fed and watered him slowly, somewhat impatiently. Soon, he was lucid and asked me where I had gone.

I told Ross that was "none of your business, MacDonald. Rest, and I will be back in a few hours, likely before midnight."

"The witching hour," he whispered.

I smiled, again showing my incisors, now retracted. I nodded, said, "Yes, the witching hour."

✝

Leaving my prisoner chained, I returned to Cate who was standing beside the horse, talking to it. As I approached her, the horse stomped its left hoof and bared its teeth in my direction which was reminiscent of Byron's dog, Boomer barking and growling at me when I first became a vampyre. However, when Cate stroked the horse's mane, the animal became docile. She looked at me, said, "Oh how odd, he was so calm."

"He is fine now."

We then proceeded to the Royal Theatre to enjoy Shakespeare's *Romeo and Juliet*. I asked Cate as we took our box seat, "Have you ever seen this play?"

She shook her head, replied, "No, but I have read it."

"Wonderful," I said, then added, "I have neither seen nor read it."

"Oh, you will very much enjoy this play, and I am sure, this production."

We settled back to revel in Shakespeare's romantic tragedy. Cate took my left hand in hers when Juliet stabbed herself with Romeo's dagger because her love, Romeo, was dead. Cate squeezed my hand and whispered, "Oh."

Outside the Royal theatre as we stepped into the carriage, Cate explained she had not realized how powerfully sad that moment would be on stage. "I almost could not catch my breath."

I nodded, asked her, "Are you hungry?" I had practiced this question early in the day only so I would remember to ask, especially after I had forgotten to feed and water MacDonald.

She smiled, "A little, yes. Are you?"

I decided not to lie, so I admitted that I was not hungry, but "I am thirsty, yes." I looked down Lothian Street and did not immediately note an eating establishment. I suggested we drive the rig for a few city blocks and see if we might find a cafe or pub. "Would you mind going into a pub, Cate?"

"No, not when I am with you, John."

I remembered telling my father the lie that I was falling in love with Elizabeth Talbot. If my father asked me now if I was falling in love with Catherine Ferguson, I believe my response would be "yes" and that it would be truthful.

We found a small quiet tavern not far from the theatre. The sign above the door read, *The Foxes' Den*. We were seated by the front window at a table for two. Because no wine was listed on the menu, I ordered a mead, hoping I might tolerate it. Cate ordered a small bowl of beef stew with rye bread and butter and an ale. She whispered, "I prefer ale over mead." Her blue eyes sparkled. I touched the top of her right hand, then leaned down to kiss it.

She giggled, joked, "Why John, so forward in public!"

At first, I did not know her meaning until I saw her wink. Then, I grinned, accidentally showing my retracted incisors ever so briefly. Cate did not gasp, but she pulled her hand from the table and put it firmly in her lap. She studied my eyes, then sighed. She said, "I must be tired. I am seeing things." Then, she leaned forward and asked me in a quiet, private voice, "I have wondered, John, how you lost your hand."

"Oh, that." And for a moment, I could not recall the story I had decided made the most sense. I remembered telling someone, *oh Sir William or was it Andrea Vaccà*, that a tiger mauled me and caused the loss of my right surgical hand and forearm. Then, abruptly, I remembered. I had told my mother the *correct story. But what is it?* I looked helplessly at Cate. I cleared my throat.

She put her hand back on the table, searching for my left hand. "Never mind that, John. You will tell me whenever you are ready."

Relieved, I thanked her. I sipped the mead cautiously while she ate her beef stew, rye bread, and drank her ale much faster than I drank my mead. She kept studying me, and I attempted to remain impassable. Finally, when she had had enough food and drink, she looked out at the dark, virtually empty street and said, "Oh my, how late it is. We need to get on the road to Dean Village."

✝

Coming back from Dean Village to my house in Charlotte Square close to midnight, the moon shone darker than I had ever seen it with streaks of red crossing its surface. In the darkness, I drove the horse slowly, watching out for the deep ruts in the unpaved roadway while shadows danced before my eyes. I was happier than I had been since before Mungo bit me, but I was also extremely tired. I was happy because Cate and I had kissed again on her porch and I knew she wanted to invite me into her home even though she did not. I was tired because I had struggled since I had had the small amount of mead at *The Foxes' Den*. I had struggled because the mead caused me to recognize that I was thirsty, not for water but for blood. Therefore, while standing on Cate's porch, holding her body close to mine, her blood scent had been so overwhelmingly powerful that I was forced to work in a way I had *never* worked to resist my natural instinct to bite her in the neck, and take blood at least from her jugular vein. Now, driving the carriage, I was shifting my attention from Cate's blood scent to Ross MacDonald's. I knew that when I entered my house, my first task would be to bite the boy. My fear was that I would not resist taking blood from his carotid artery which would more than likely kill him. I did not want to kill Ross. I needed him if I was to continue to court Cate Ferguson as *a man rather than a vampyre*. And so, I drove in the dark in fear.

✝

I slept very late into Sunday morning after arriving home after midnight, after *the witching hour*. I had gone into the root cellar which was in total darkness. I had located the single gas lamp, turned the cock, and lit a match. With the igniting of the gas and the resulting light, I saw that Ross had found his legs. He was standing up, leaning against the post, the irons around his ankles and wrists intact, the chain secure. He had managed to get to his knees and then stand, I presumed. He seemed calm, so I said, "Good evening, Ross."

"Good morning, John."

I was so fatigued, I did not chuckle at Ross' wit as I usually would have. Instead, I approached the young man, pulled his collar away from his neck, and bit him even as he tried to kick my shins and push against my chest with his chained limbs. I had allowed him more freedom of movement than I had realized, but he did not hurt me, he only annoyed me as he had before.

Though I had bitten him, I had not yet begun to pull blood from the boy, so I took my mouth from his neck, retracted my incisors, and said sharply, "Stop that, MacDonald. Stop that now. I am too tired to fight you."

"Get on with it then," he said, dejected and angry.

"I promise," I said softly, "I won't turn you and I won't kill you."

"I wish you *would* kill me," he said with bitterness.

I bit him then, taking enough blood from his jugular vein that I would be satisfied at least until the morning. The boy cried as I drank and I wished I could shut up my ears.

When I finished and was ready to turn down the gas and shut the cock of the lamp, Ross begged me for "water and something, anything to eat."

Growing up in Soho, I had not had a pet. I was not familiar with the need to tend to an animal. I needed to think of Ross as an animal, nay a pet who was completely dependent upon me, his owner, his master. I nodded, said that I would be back.

I did as I had done earlier in the evening before going to the theatre with Cate. I brought Ross water, cheeses, and bread. As I was exiting the root cellar, the young man said, "This won't do over time, you know, John. You'll have to give me something more substantial or you will have a corpse down here rather than a man to feed upon."

"Good point, Ross. Thank you."

And I turned off the gas lamp, and went straightaway to bed.

✝

The next day, I began to court Cate in earnest. Every chance which presented itself was a chance to spend more time in her presence. Some week's ends, we took long carriage rides into the countryside. Sometimes we visited other villages near to Edinburgh. At other times, we enjoyed boat tours along the Water of Leith river. Over several months, we took in every museum in Edinburgh where Cate proved more knowledgable than myself on occasion.

In the evenings when I left her on her front porch, our kisses became more and more passionate, and if not for the blood of Ross MacDonald I am sure that I would have taken Cate's blood without any reservations.

Finally, I risked telling Cate that I loved her. And my heart leapt when she shyly said, "I love you as well, John Monro."

✝

Once we declared our love, the next step I took with great care. I invited Cate into my home in Charlotte Square after drinking a significant amount of Ross' blood and then securing him with a cloth gag and warning him to "be utterly quiet."

In the dining room upstairs, Cate and I then indulged in a superb dinner during which I tried to eat various foods without success, explaining to my companion that my stomach "appears out of sorts." Cate accepted my excuse for we had not eaten together since our theatre outing. Of course, for this evening, I had paired the excellent foodstuffs with several wine choices which I *was* able to enjoy. Afterwards, I began to show Cate the house, finally ending our tour in the master bathroom. When Cate saw the tub, the glowing embers in the fireplace, and the steaming kettle of water, she laughed. She looked at me, playfully pinched my right upper arm, above the elbow, and whispered, "I cannot believe it."

"Believe it," I said. Then I reached out carefully, began to unbutton her high collar with my left hand. I watched Cate's round, soft face for any sign of embarrassment or distaste. I saw only expressions of love and trust. *Trust?* I wondered how it was possible that I had gained the trust of this intelligent schoolmistress. I cautiously turned her around and slid her bodice off her shoulders. From behind her, while I slowly unlaced her corset, I whispered, "Go ahead, take a bath. I will pour the water for you, while it remains hot, and leave you alone." Cate beamed. In complete comfort, she began to undress even before I exited as I had planned to provide her privacy. With her back turned, she continued to step out of her linen dress and her shift worn next to her skin. While Cate was so occupied, I used my extraordinary strength to lift the kettle and repeatedly pour enough hot water directly into the tub for the woman I loved to enjoy the luxury of a hot bath. If Cate noticed my inordinate strength, she said nothing. Then, I stepped from the bathroom.

While Cate bathed alone, I removed my clothing, hanging the various items on the bedposts, then I stretched out on my bed, and waited with remarkable patience, given that the vampyre appeared content to leave me alone. I wondered if it would be as content to leave Cate alone when she appeared. I waited.

As I hoped, twenty minutes later, Cate exited the master bathroom naked except for a towel draped around her waist. Her bare breasts glistened with moisture while her long and curling wet hair covered her shoulders. As soon as I saw her, my physical reactions were all too human. The vampyre remained quiet. *Thank God,* I whispered. I patted the mattress, and Cate came to me, smiling. I stood up to kiss her, removing the towel so that I might press myself into her. We briefly parted so that I might position her gently on the bed. There, in a quiet and fully human passion, completely unlike the vampyre's night with the whore, Cate and I consummated our love.

Chapter Twenty: Mary

Unbeknownst to me during my time courting Cate while continuing to consume blood from my prisoner, Ross MacDonald, Mary, who had married Percy Shelley, and Claire, who had married Lord Byron, had taken leave of their husbands temporarily in an effort to locate their friend, Doctor John Polidori.

Mary had always been a highly intelligent woman, so it is not surprising to me that she found me by contacting my parents in Soho. Of course, my father Gaetano and my mother, Anna Maria knew Mrs. Shelley and had at least heard of Lady Claire Clairmont Byron. Therefore, of course, my parents informed my two well known, well loved friends that I was currently living in Charlotte Square and teaching anatomy at the University of Edinburgh. Mary especially expressed shock that her friend had returned to Scotland. She had expected me to be in Italy or Greece, researching my story, *The Vampyre* while practicing medicine. Mary had not been convinced that Claire's story about John Polidori was entirely accurate for how could vampyres exist? She secretly believed that perhaps Claire had imagined much, perhaps all of what had happened on Lake Geneva.

On the other hand, Claire had thought, at first, that I might have turned so far into monster as to have become lost in the forests of Switzerland. If she had been privy to the headline in the newspaper of Papal Rome, she might have realized I was still alive and taking blood from human beings. Claire did hear about the terror of Old Town during which whores and rabble were being drained of blood, but her husband, Lord Byron forbade his wife, Lady Byron from traipsing about the slums of Edinburgh "looking for a ghost" especially when the murders abruptly stopped. Mary had been the one who had first grown alarmed when neither she nor Claire had heard from me in what seemed too many months, then years. Claire later confessed that her fear of me had been so powerful, so overwhelming that it deterred her from searching for me and only Mary's insistence convinced her that I needed finding. Claire then laid down specific rules for the visit to Charlotte Square, and Mary had reluctantly agreed.

While my friends were surprised at my current location, what at first bewildered me is that my father did not write to inform me that my friends were coming to visit. I know now that Mary and Claire asked him not to inform me, that they wished to "surprise John."

✝

When Mary Shelley and Claire Byron knocked on my front door at 1 Great Stuart Street in Charlotte Square and I answered, they were confused by my appearance. Although the young man before them was familiar, he was *not* John Polidori.

Mary, somewhat shocked, said, "Oh, excuse us." And she looked me up and down. When she spotted my short right extremity, she was thoroughly confused. "Are you Dr. Polidori?"

"No, I am not. My name is Alex, Alex Monro."

Claire, stepping forward, spat, "You lie."

Mary looked at her friend and stepsister, upset. "What are you doing, Claire?"

"It *is* John, Mary."

I must have blushed, for Mary stepped closer to me, and said, "I think you are right, Claire. How is this possible?" Then she spoke to me again, "John?"

And, in that moment, I could tell I had lost the characteristics of Alex that I worked so hard to maintain. As I predicted, transforming only parts of myself while leaving others intact, required a great deal of energy. As I involuntarily turned into myself, I whispered, "Mary, Claire, please come in. I can explain."

Claire pulled from a pocket in her skirt a rather large gold crucifix and held it in both hands before her. "We will come in, John, but beware. I know what you are."

I laughed, but secretly was pleased to see that Claire had the wherewithal to protect herself and Mary. I was relieved that although the large crucifix repelled me, so that I was forced to step backwards into my foyer, it did not seem to harm me, at least not yet. Then, I asked my friends to enter Alexander Monro Tertius' home. I told them to take seats in the parlor and even offered them a pot of tea and a tray of biscuits, the biscuits Sir William had recommended so enthusiastically. I think my dear friend Claire did not expect me to have any humanity. She seemed to believe I would be only monster by now, more than two years after Mungo's bite had changed me. *I am a monster. I have imprisoned a boy in the root cellar, a boy I treat like a blood bag.* I sat down on the sofa across from my friends when they both declined my offer of tea, smiled rather feebly.

Mary asked me, "John, how have you been?"

"Terrible, Mary." But then I thought of Cate, who I had visited in her cottage in the night before my friends' unexpected arrival. Cate and I had consummated our love once again, this time in her small bed in her cozy bedroom. I had left her only a few hours ago. Therefore, I stared directly at Claire whose blood urgently called to me. I whispered, "Yet, wonderful." I could see the confusion in Mary's expression. But, Claire clutched the gold crucifix tighter and glared at me. Mary turned, asked her stepsister to put the cross away. While I retained the ability, I quickly protested, "No, Claire, do not put the crucifix in your pocket or on the table there. Keep it firmly in your hands. I will kill Mary and take you prisoner if you do not." I began to weep.

Mary looked shocked. Claire only nodded because she already knew the truth. She knew *I am damned to Hell.*

I abruptly stood, which frightened Claire. I sat down again and said, "Right now, I have a prisoner in Alex's root cellar. If you will allow me, I will go downstairs and release him. He may be too weak to flee, but if I can, I will put him upstairs in a bed and let him recover himself. I have not turned him into vampyre nor have I killed him, most obviously. I have been feeding off him now for several months." I wavered, said, "Maybe longer. I am not sure."

"Oh John," cried Mary, but Claire nodded. She said, "Free him, John. Should I go with you, carrying the crucifix so you will not change your mind." She said it like a statement rather than a question, so I nodded. Then I warned them both, "You will be shocked at what I have done, at what I am doing." I sighed. "But I have a reason that is not *entirely* evil. I have fallen in love and to keep from drinking her blood, I have done this thing in the root cellar."

Claire said coldly, "We shall see."

Her blood scent, as it had always been for me, was overwhelmingly attractive, pulling me towards her even as the crucifix in her hands repulsed me. I whispered, "Hold it tightly, Claire. I can be very quick when I want to be. Very quick."

"I appreciate your warning, John. I do indeed." And she clutched the cross ever so tightly to her breast. "Let us see this person you have imprisoned."

We proceeded to the root cellar. When I lit the gas lamp, the light illuminated a young man who now was more little boy than the intelligent and handsome medical student I had first met. He whimpered as I approached to unchain him. He whispered most hoarsely, "Please, John, please, no."

I whispered back, "No, Ross, I am letting you go." He looked at me with total disbelief and said as much. "Ross, I am not lying. I am letting you go. Be still now, and I will release your bonds."

As I approached the boy, my mind protested, *if you release him, you condemn Cate. I will take her. I will.* I shook my head with every intention of unlocking Ross' chains. But MacDonald began to struggle, slapping at me with his chained arms. I turned to Mary, "Would you?" And I showed her the key that I kept around my neck. I pulled it off and started to reach out with the intention of giving it to my friend. I changed my mind and warned again, "Do not approach me, Mary. I will put the key here on the floor and back away. Wait for me to reach that wall there, then pick up the key. Claire, you keep the crucifix tightly in your hands where I can always see and feel it. Otherwise, I will kill Mary, as I said before."

Mary began to shake. Whereas she had not been afraid, she was now. I watched as the terrified woman took the key from the blood soaked floor, put it into the shackles at the boy's ankles and turned it so that the irons fell away. Ross' ankles were raw and bleeding. Mary then unlocked the wrist irons and the boy's wrists were in even worse shape. The boy's fresh blood made me feel like a trapped animal. I pressed myself into the wall and kept my eyes affixed on the cross Claire held in front of her breast.

Ross was unable to stand. Contrary to my promise to put my victim into a bed, I realized that I could not approach him. If I did, I would, without meaning to do so, transform into the lion, swipe the crucifix from Claire's grip, and maul all three of these human beings to death. I would not save a one of them, not even Claire. I decided to tell the truth. "I cannot help you, Mary. You must take the boy upstairs, put him in any bedroom but the one with the adjoining bath. I am not sure you can lock the door from the outside, but I think I can leave the boy alone if his blood scent is far from me."

Mary pondered aloud, "Blood scent?"

"I will explain everything later," I said.

Claire said, "I know what that means, John."

155

I looked at her and nodded, "Yes, I am sure you do since it is your blood I lust after every day of my existence now."

"Since you first bit me," she said.

"Yes," I whispered. I looked at Mary. "Try to get Ross upstairs now."

✝

Mary struggled to help Ross up the steep stairs out of the cellar. She stumbled several times, but finally managed to get the boy into the back kitchen where she took a moment to wash his face, hands and feet with cool water from the ice box. Then, she began the long and tedious struggle to get the boy up the main staircase and into a bedroom. Finally, she returned to the parlor, saying quietly to Claire, "I think he is all right. I put the boy to bed." Then, she whispered, "He looks so frightened and so weak. Poor child."

Claire never even glanced at Mary. Instead she kept her eyes fixed on me, the gold crucifix still held in front of her. I had come up from the cellar along with her. After Mary had left the root cellar with Ross MacDonald, I had instructed Claire to insist that I go first while she followed behind. In reality, neither way we exited the cellar would have made any real difference. Either way, I would not have seen the crucifix that Claire held. But if I was in front of her, I could not turn around and attack her, for then I would see the crucifix and its presence would repel me. So, the man in me opted to insist to Claire that I go up the steep stairs first and she follow me.

Therefore while trudging slowly up the steep stairwell, I was required to resist running full out. I knew I could escape, but I feared I would escape only to go upstairs to the bedrooms, locate and kill Ross and then Mary, and finally imprison Claire if I could. I did not wish to do this, so I had obediently gone into the parlor and had sat down under Claire's watchful eyes.

✝

Now that Mary had joined myself and Claire and informed us that Ross likely would need a long recovery, I asked my friends, "Now what?"

Claire said, "Mary and I have an idea we believe will work."

"What's that?" I asked again.

Mary swallowed, began, "We are going to perform an exorcism."

I laughed heartily, the evil in me showing. I bared my teeth, extending my incisors, and literally growled at Mary. Mary almost fainted. I calmed myself, said, "I am sorry, Mary. Please try to forgive me." Then, I looked at Claire, said, "I do not see how that will work. I cannot even enter a churchyard much less a church."

"We plan to bring the priest here," said Claire because Mary had begun to vomit uncontrollably onto the floor and even the table in front of her.

"Honestly, Claire, I am afraid you will not be able to contain me much longer. I am growing hungry." I added, "And when I am blood deprived, that is when my human will power weakens."

Claire nodded, "I suspected something like that. The priest should be here momentarily."

I raised my eyebrows, looked at the woman whose blood pulled at me, and said, "You are a wise woman, Claire Clairmont."

"Byron," she said.

"Oh sure," I said. "I forgot about old George, deliberately." And I smiled, showing my incisors, still fully extended.

Chapter Twenty One: Platitude

Sure enough, within moments of Mary and Claire announcing their plan, which to my vampyre heart and mind seemed ridiculously naive and even childish, my front door rattled with a rapid series of sturdy, insistent knocking.

"That is the priest, now," said Claire. "Come with me, John. We will let him in together."

"I would rather wait, here."

Claire actually smiled at me as if I was a child. She said, "I am sure you would, but obviously, you must come with me. You said yourself you need to be in sight of and able to feel the crucifix of our Lord and Savior, Jesus Christ."

When she said the words "Lord and Savior, Jesus Christ," it was as if she had struck me in the chest, this time with a dull mallet or a sharp axe. I momentarily buckled in enormous pain. I panted.

Mary, who had recovered, asked, "John. Are you all right?"

I shook my head, said, "I have not been all right since the day in that carriage when Mungo bit me."

Mary seemed embarrassed as she mumbled, "Of course, John. I cannot imagine the horrors of the past years." Then, she blushed, asked, "You said you fell in love. Who is she whom you love?"

Before I could answer, another series of sharp knocks came against Alex's front door. I rose. "Come on," I said to Claire, "let us get this farce over with."

"Not a farce, John. Not by any means."

"I honestly hope not," I said, tears forming in my eyes, unexpectedly.

Claire and I walked to the front door. I stood against the wall, facing Claire and the crucifix still firmly held in both her hands. She noted that I was watching, like the big cat hunter, like the vampyre I was, for any weakness, any sign of inattention, any opportunity to strike. Of course, I had had *many* opportunities but I was working diligently to avoid taking advantage of these which required a great deal of energy and will power.

Claire opened the door, and welcomed the Roman Catholic priest into Alex Monro's house. The priest immediately identified himself as "the exorcist." I laughed, deliberately revealing my, at the present, retracted incisors to the man as he crossed the threshold into the foyer. I noted that he did not appear to be particularly afraid of me, likely because he had never beheld a creature like myself.

I said to him, "Good evening, Father."

He nodded, said, "Good evening." Then, he glanced at Claire.

She warned, "Be careful, Father. He is more dangerous than he appears. He can change form in an instant, tear out a throat, or bite your neck and drink all your blood in a moment out of time. He may even be able to transform you into what he is."

The priest looked at the young woman, my friend, who had written to him about a doctor who required an exorcism, and asked, "What is he?"

I stepped forward, then stepped away from the crucifixes. One was held by Claire and the other was around the priest's neck, hanging near his breastbone right beside his heart. I cleared my throat, said, "I am a vampyre, Father."

The priest smiled, nodded. "A vampyre?"

"I know," I whispered, "we do not exist."

"No, not that I am aware of," said the exorcist, still smiling at me. "More likely, you suffer from a demon masquerading as a vampyre."

I admitted to myself that his theory was ingenious though incorrect. I smiled back, again showing him my now fully extended, elongated, and sharp incisors. The priest stepped back and I stepped forward. "I am what I say I am, priest. I am a vampyre and it is only because I do not wish to kill Mary Shelley and imprison Claire Clairmont, excuse me, Byron that I have not already killed you." And I growled at the man who shrunk back against the closed door.

Claire interrupted our exchange, and suggested that we "get started."

The exorcist now appeared terrified, reaching back for the handle that would open the front door and allow his escape. He said to Claire, "Missus Byron, I do not believe I am fully prepared to deal with this unholy situation. I wish you had been more upfront with me in your letters." Claire then clutched the exorcist's right arm, letting go of the crucifix with her left hand, and said sharply, "If you leave us, John *will* kill Mary and a boy upstairs and then he will make me his own, forever."

When Claire let go of the crucifix with one hand, the vampyre in me leapt forward pushing my body toward the priest, but with everything that was still human in me, I resisted. I held him back, and said, "Missus Byron speaks the truth. I am rapidly losing my ability to withhold my innate desire to kill you all, except that I will do everything in my power *not* to kill Claire. Claire I will keep in the root cellar for her entire life. And, I *will* extend her life if I can, first for the lust of blood, and second for the love of a woman."

The exorcist still pressing himself against the door shook his head, "I do not understand." He looked at me, and asked without expecting an answer, "How can you love?"

I laughed, "You, priest, must have faith in your God."

With that, the exorcist, suddenly and inexplicably angry, clutched the crucifix around his neck, and said, "Do not mock me or the Lord Jesus Christ, fiend."

I felt again as if I had been struck in the chest with a fireplace poker long heated in burning embers. This time, I was the one who pressed myself into the wall after falling back. I growled. The priest, who recognized that I had become, at least for the moment, the one who was afraid, stepped forward, holding the crucifix toward my face. I growled again, tried to move away. I sidled along the wall, turned my body away from the exorcist.

Claire realized that I was in enormous physical pain. She said, "Our Lord and Savior, Jesus Christ commands you, demon, to leave John Polidori now." Her words stung as if thousands of hornets had attacked every inch of my skin. I twisted my face, and growled at her. Then, I put my back to both Claire and the priest, pressing my face into the wall. The exorcist said to Claire, "Very good, child. Very good." I could not see him for I was cowering. I heard him whisper to her, "Together, now." In unison, Claire and the exorcist began to recite the Lord's Prayer, a prayer I had grown up reciting with my mother, Anna Maria and father, Gaetano, with my sibling brothers and sisters, with my parish priest in the confessional, and at mass. I cried out. A moment later, I heard Mary Shelley's voice as she joined Claire and the priest. Together with the exorcist's guidance, I recognized that they had begun to pray the rosary. Yet, it seemed only the words "Our Lord and Savior, Jesus Christ" possessed power against me. Perhaps only the words "Jesus Christ?" Or perhaps only the word "Christ?" Even though I recognized that those were *the words* that hurt, I could not think *those words*. However, I was able to muse, *How many times growing up did I hear his name used in passing, in vain? How many times did I myself use his name in vain?*

When Claire abruptly said the Christ's name again, I felt as if I was literally on fire, as if in a moment I might be reduced to a pathetic pile of ashes. And, his name, each time I heard it, was a stake driven into my very soul. I could feel the truth, *I am dying.* Because I was so much nearer to death than I had thought possible, I growled, twisted my body around, and scratched at the wall in front of my face, and at the floor at my feet, utterly desperate. I thought, *Finally God, you are paying attention to me. You are stopping me, finally you are punishing me. Lord, Finally.* And then I marveled that the generic words, *God* and *Lord* did not hurt in the least.

Then, most unfortunately at that critical moment, I heard a typically ineffectual platitude from the priest. He boldly said, "No, John, the Lord loves you."

I laughed for I knew that was a lie. *Your God does not love me.* I laughed heartily but with sadness once more. The exorcist's platitude was highly amusing because ironically *My Lord is Satan and I know without a doubt he does not love me, that he is utterly incapable of love.*

Therefore, with this priest's worthless platitude, I had immediately regained the advantage, if only for a moment. I spun my body around to turn on the man with every intention of tearing out his throat in the form of the male lion, but Claire, with both hands, thrust her crucifix between me and the exorcist. Claire's crucifix stopped my transformation into lion. Her action prevented me from killing the man, and everyone else except Claire, while the priest's stationary crucifix around his neck did not. Defeated for the moment, I sat on the floor, leaned against the wall. I relaxed. Then, I lied. I said to my friends and the exorcist, "I am done. It is finished."

Claire looked at me. She started to relax along with me, lowering her hands with the crucifix still clutched in them. I looked back at her, tried to tell her to be careful, but I could not speak. Claire looked at me again, said, "John, look at me." I did not. She said it again, "John. John, look at me." Again, I did not raise my eyes to hers. She wisely sensed that I was not myself yet, and warned, "Do not believe him, Father. He lies." I thought, *you, Claire, know me better than anyone, certainly better than Mary, even better than Cate, and certainly better than this exorcist.*

The priest, sorely afraid, tensed and clutched his own crucifix as he studied the man before him. I could see that he wanted to escape, but he just stood with his back against Alex's front door.

Now, we have reached an impasse, albeit a temporary one, for I will win.

The exorcist, virtually trapped in Alex Monro's foyer, was utterly exhausted, lacking faith in his ability to harness the power of God to overcome the power of Satan that continued to reside within me, that continued its almost total power over my body and soul.

I knew without a doubt that eventually *I will win over Heaven* for the vampyre in me was incredibly powerful. I recognized with horror that the priest, who was ill equipped as exorcist, would not succeed. I knew that I would soon kill this pathetic man before me. I would then kill Mary, kill Ross next, and finally begin to consume Claire's blood, a goal, *the goal* I had had since I first tasted her in Villa Diodati that strange June.

And with even more horror, I envisioned my legal, not holy marriage to Cate Ferguson, condemning her to a life with an evil thing that would in the end destroy her. I would not age while she grew older, feeble and *ugly*, I thought. Eventually, I would tire of her loss of beauty and youth. I would then begin to take her blood, slowly at first, while she slept next to me, then I would take more and more of her blood until I would want another woman, a younger, more beautiful version. So I would seek out another to replace Cate. Finally, perhaps reluctantly, I would kill my wife by biting her carotid artery and draining all the blood from the woman I now claimed to love.

I sat on the cold floor in the foyer of Alexander Monro Tertius' home, and began to weep, nearly uncontrollably. My vision of my eternal future on this earth had depressed me and I recognized that I was truly tired, utterly weary of *this life.*

Yet, I also was incredibly hungry. *The blood lust will win unless a change occurs.* Soon the man in me would be silenced, and the vampyre would gain and keep the upper hand. *Something has to change and now.* I could not say, nay even think *the words* that needed to be said, so I glanced at Mary, whispered hoarsely before the vampyre could steal my voice, "The words." She leaned in toward me at which time Claire shouted a terse warning, "Get back, Mary." But Mary ignored Claire. She leaned in ever closer, risking her very life, and asked, "What did you say, John?"

I once more whispered hoarsely while I still retained a measure of human strength, "The words, Mary, the words."

"What words, John?"

Claire raised her eyebrows in sudden recognition of what I meant. She said, "Oh Mary, it is too simple!"

Mary stared at her friend, "What?"

With boldness I had always admired in this young woman, Claire stood up, raised the gold crucifix over my head while I still sat exhausted and weeping against the wall. I felt some hope. The young woman, whose blood I still lusted for, began to steadily repeat Christ's name over and over and over until I felt as if my whole body would explode. Every fiber of my being ached, screaming *pain* in a way I had never experienced. I cried, I growled, I tried in vain to transform. Then, I began to profusely bleed from my ears, from my eyes, from my nose, from my mouth. I tried to stand, but could not. I tried to lie down, but could not. I tried to press myself into the wall behind me, but could not. I reached out, attempting to snatch the crucifix from the grip of Claire, but I stopped myself from doing so. I knew I could still win the battle, but I also knew *I do not want to win. I want to lose.* I wanted to let go of the curse, to abandon the horrid yet wondrous powers of Hell and choose Heaven, and it did not matter what Heaven would bring to me. Heaven might mean my death, or it might mean my earthly salvation. Heaven might mean something entirely different, utterly unknown. Since I did not know, I did not care. Once more, I began to cry, my tears mixing with the warm blood continuing to flow from my orifices.

As Claire continued to repeat the name of the Christ, everything began to release, and finally I felt the vampyre leave me. The pains ceased, the bleeding began to subside. I sat quite still, perplexed, then fearful, then I began to feel the relief like a slow tide coming in after a storm. I waited, fully expecting the vampyre to make his appearance and take my body back. Claire, however, was still speaking the name of the Christ, over and over and over. I looked at her and weakly smiled. Claire stopped chanting, studied me carefully, lowered the crucifix, the holding of which had caused her hands to cramp, and began to cry. Then, she started laughing. She reached down and touched my wet cheek. I looked up at her. She whispered, "Hello, John. Hello there, dear John."

"Claire!" I said as I had not seen her in over two years.

Chapter Twenty-Two: Dying

Mary, Claire, and the priest helped me to my feet, guided me into the parlor where they assisted me onto the sofa. I leaned back in a state of both wonder and confusion. Slowly, I began to remember who I had been and who I was now. I sat straight up in utter surprise despite immense physical weakness. I licked my lips, touched my teeth with my tongue. *Ordinary teeth,* I thought, laughing out loud. I looked at Claire, nearly shouted, "Ordinary teeth. Look, Claire. My teeth! They are just like yours!" Then, I collapsed backwards onto the cushions behind my back. I lost consciousness.

Claire explained later how she had become alarmed by my sudden physical weakness, an odd change in my appearance, and a strange giddiness. What she, Mary, and the priest did not realize, at least at first, was that, immediately after the vampyre abandoned my body, I aged slightly more than two years in seconds. Additionally, I was starving to death right before their eyes. I had not consumed human food in more than nine months and even the food I had consumed in the months prior I usually had vomited out of my body. My body, now fully human and older, which had expelled a great deal of blood while the vampyre was exiled from me, was wasting away in front of them.

When I regained consciousness because Mary had placed a cool cloth on my forehead while stroking my black hair, I also did not fully understand why my body was reacting this way. As I sat under the touch of Mary's kind hands, I remembered that I had been bleeding from every facial orifice and had felt like I was losing bulk, which I presumed was primarily muscle. Now, I seemed close to death. I looked at Mary in desperation. I whispered, "Tell Cate I love her."

Mary stopped stroking my hair, and asked, "Who?"

"Cate Ferguson," I said softly. "She lives in Dean Village. She is a schoolmistress there." Then, with relief, I said, "I never bit her, Mary." I turned to Claire, pleading, "I never bit her, not even once. That is why I treated Ross so terribly." And I began to weep again. All the guilt and shame flooded over me despite my joy at having been set free of the vampyre. I looked at Mary, continued, "I had hunted for a young woman like Cate, a woman from whom the vampyre could take blood routinely, but I fell in love. So, I captured and drank from Ross so that I could escape the blood lust I would naturally feel with Cate."

"I promise," said Mary, nodding as if she understood. "I will tell her."

"And please," I begged, "do not tell her what I was. Please. I do not think she knows. I would like it if she remembers me the way I am now, as John." I smiled, explained, "Cate called me John." My friends looked confused, so I said, "A nickname. I told her it was my childhood nickname given to me by my mother." I smiled weakly. "One of the few things I told her that was *not* a lie."

The priest interrupted, declared, "You can tell her yourself. You are not going to die."

"Die? Are you dying, John?" Claire asked, seemingly unaware of the poor state of my human body. She became immensely distressed.

I nodded, whispered, "I think I *am* dying, Claire. I am so sorry for everything."

The priest shook his head. He looked at the two young women, and commanded them both to "find anything he can eat. Now!" Neither Mary nor Claire was offended. Instead, each looked to the other. Claire said, "We went through a kitchen to get to the root cellar." Both immediately headed to Alex's back kitchen and returned not long after with a platter upon which were spread the cheeses, breads, and butter. I also had recently purchased fruit for Ross, so apple and pear pieces were scattered on the platter as well. While Claire handled the platter, Mary carried a large pitcher of water. Mary said to the priest, "All of this food was in the ice box, but none is very cold. Most of the ice block is melted."

"That is all right," said the man. "Let us move John into the dining room where we can help him to eat." Then he paused, asked, "Did you say there's a boy upstairs?"

Mary nodded. "Oh yes. The poor boy! Shall I try to bring him down?"

The exorcist said, "No, go up and check on him, please." The man hesitated, added, "And take the young man some food and water!"

"Of course," replied Mary, but she did not leave. She stared at me. I could see lines of worry and fear on her face. I whispered, "Go on, Mary. See to MacDonald." When I said the boy's surname, I began to weep.

As Mary left the foyer, the priest commanded me, "Come with us." In response, I tried to stand, but Claire and the man had to assist me to the dining table. I collapsed into a chair, then Claire sat next to me. She cut small pieces of the various cheeses, of the two fruits, then of the two breads and fed each to me as I was helpless. After only a few bites, I knew I was going to vomit if she gave me more, so I put my left hand against Claire's arm as she attempted to feed me another bite of apple.

At that moment, Mary returned to us and smiled when she saw me in the dining room and eating. She said cheerfully, "Ross is awake. He is all right, I believe." She smiled again. "No, I mean he is going to recover. I talked with him more. He had improved lucidity, and he was able to eat and drink a little." We all felt relief, although a deep worry lingered in me.

As Claire attempted to give me the piece of apple that I had resisted, I whispered, "Water for now, Claire. Just water." The priest was suddenly suspicious, so I assured him, "I am myself, Father." Then, I studied the man, a stranger, asked, "Who are you?"

The priest smiled. "My name is Father Charles McIntosh."

I smiled in return. "My name is John Polidori."

"A pleasure to meet you, John."

I looked at Charles McIntosh, and whispered, "Will you hear my confession, Father?"

Father McIntosh nodded, "Yes." And he smiled broadly as if incredibly relieved. "Yes, John for it is long past time that you unburdened yourself."

I agreed. I cried like a little boy who had been found and led home after a long and hard absence.

Chapter Twenty-Three: Restitution

Seven months later when I was sufficiently recovered, gaining some weight and beginning to enjoy the consumption of several foods, I took aside Mrs. Mary Shelley who had remained with me in the Monro house in Charlotte Square while Lady Claire had returned to her husband, Lord George Byron in London. I spoke quietly to Mary, "I need to travel to Rome."

"Whatever for?"

"To find Doctor Alexander Monro Tertius, and restore him to his house and position at the university if at all possible."

"I will come with you," she said.

At first, I protested, but quickly relented when Mary insisted. She also suggested that Percy, Claire, and even George "join us."

"Maybe not George," I said, smiling sheepishly.

Mary looked at me, and said, "Yes, maybe not Lord Byron." She paused, added softly, "He *was* unusually mean to you that terrible summer at Villa Diodati, wasn't he?"

I nodded, "Yes, he was." I hesitated, said, "But first, I must go to Dean Village and explain to Cate why she has neither heard from nor seen me in all these long months."

"What will you tell her?" Mary asked. "Do you want me to come along? Perhaps it would help if I was with you."

"I do not believe Cate will even see me," I admitted. "I have not even bothered to write her a letter."

"John," Mary exclaimed, "you have been at death's door for so long now. You are just now regaining your strength. You still barely eat!" Then, she brightened, suggested, "Why not allow me to write Miss Ferguson?"

"Would you?"

"Of course, John."

So, Mary Shelley, the present and future author of the skillfully written horror tale, *Frankenstein*, sat at Monro's oak desk upstairs and composed a beautiful letter to Catherine Ferguson.

Dear Miss Ferguson,

You do not know me, so allow me to introduce myself. My name is Mary Shelley, married now almost a year and a half to the poet, Mister Percy Shelley of some renown in England. More to the point, I am also a dear friend of the man you know of as Alexander Monro Tertius and whom you call "John."

I realize that the following may come as a shock, so do prepare yourself. I am certain that you are presently hurting and perhaps angry because you have not heard or seen John in nearly a year.

Let me assure you that John has been near death and unable to even write to you. This is the reason this letter is penned by me rather than by John himself.

Let me also assure you that John is not going to die. He is recovering and hopes that you will receive him sooner than later. He needs to return to Rome on an errand of much importance. I am to travel with him as the loving and loyal friend that I have been for years. Several others will join us in Rome. When we return to Scotland, I do hope and trust that you will receive John and myself at your home in Dean Village.

In the meantime, please pray that we have safe travels and accomplish our holy task.

With utmost kind regards,

Mrs. Mary Wollstonecraft Godwin Shelley

I read Mary's writing, and wept. Then I penned in poor, nearly illegible script, *I love and miss you, Cate. Yours always, John.*

Mary posted the letter the next morning. When she returned to the house, she said, "I thought about telling Miss Ferguson how you are *not* Alexander, but decided that is something you should explain in person."

"You are a wise woman, Mrs. Shelley."

"That undertaking will be difficult, John."

"I know." I sighed, "Very difficult."

✝

Mary then wrote two more letters, the first to her husband, Percy and the other to Lady Claire Clairmont Byron in London. While waiting for their responses by post, Mary, in contrast to her letter to Miss Ferguson, again asked me if I would like to attempt the short trip by horse and carriage to Dean Village to see Cate before our trip to Rome.

"I am sore afraid, Mary." I looked at her for comfort and advice, continued, "Cate will not even recognize me. I look very little like the man she knows as 'John.' And I will not be able to transform so that she may have some proof that I am the same John Monro she knows and loves."

"She will believe you, John."

We allowed the post a few days for our letter to arrive in Dean Village, and then, with Mary's assistance, I once more rented a carriage and single horse, slowly climbed up to the cushioned, wooden seat and asked Mary, "Are you able to drive this rig?"

She laughed, "Of course!" Mary took the reins, flicked the whip, and we were off.

This day, the sun was shining which I relished. For one of the first times in more than two years, the warmth of the sun's rays did not sting my skin. I felt like a young man on a lovely and joyful summer's outing. If I had not been a vampyre and done so many horrific, evil deeds, I would have had no care in all the world on this day.

Not more than one half hour later, Mary stopped the carriage at Cate's cottage. "Stay here," she said. "I will knock on her door, and check her disposition."

"Yes," I said.

Mary climbed down from the seat, walked to the little front porch where Cate and I had kissed so many times. I watched my friend as she knocked on the wooden door. A few seconds passed, then Cate, a woman I loved dearly, appeared. I could not tell her reactions to seeing Mary and then spotting a strange figure in a distant horse drawn carriage.

For a few moments, Cate and Mary soundlessly spoke. Then, Cate stepped around Mary, and began to walk toward the carriage in which I sat. I raised my shorter right arm. Cate came even closer, then she saw my face gleaming in the sunshine. She said, "Oh." Then she turned back, strolling rapidly. Once on her porch, Cate invited Mary inside her home.

I waited, quite impatiently, for a long time.

Finally, the door opened and Mary came back to the carriage, stroking the horse briefly. She looked at me, tears in her eyes. She said, "Cate refused to see you, John."

"Oh," I said.

"She does not believe me."

"What did you tell her?"

"The same as what I wrote, that you had been near death and was now recovered enough to come in person to explain yourself."

"But Cate refused?"

"Yes, she said that the man in the carriage is 'not John.' She said, 'I won't see whoever that is.' She grew quite angry, so I took my leave. I am so sorry, John."

"There's nothing to be done," I said.

"Except pray," suggested Mary.

I smiled, nodded.

✝

Several weeks later, Mary Shelley received her anticipated responses in the post, first from Claire who wrote that she would join us in Rome, "most happily." A few days later, Percy replied that "although I would rather not travel at this time, of course I will meet you, darling in Rome."

Before we left for Rome, I asked Mary to write one more letter, this one addressed to Lord Provost Sir William Arbuthnot at the University of Edinburgh. I instructed her to, as clearly and concisely as possible, inform him of my deception and that I was soon to be on my way to Italy to try to find and recover Alexander Monro Tertius to his rightful place in the world.

When I asked her to compose another letter to my former friend and mentor, Doctor Andrea Vaccà Berlinghieri to inform him of our visit, Mary advised that I not do this. She warned, "How do explain that you murdered his young female assistant, John? The good surgeon, no matter what you say or what you promise, will not understand and will not forgive you."

"You forgave me," I whispered.

"I understand and love you, John." Mary took my left hand. "But, I do not pretend to forgive you." Mary's words were like being slapped across the cheek, stinging but not causing agony as had Claire's use of the Christ's name when I had been vampyre. I nodded. We agreed that I would not call on my former friend, the surgeon.

Mary posted my letter to the Lord Provost on the day we left for Rome. We had booked passage on a sailing ship from the port of Leith to Gibraltar, changing to a different ship that we sailed from Gibraltar to the Porto di Venezia in Italy. Our entire voyage lasted five weeks, and both Mary and I were seasick over most of it. From Venice, we arranged to take a stagecoach to Papal Rome. But once we arrived in the immense and bustling city, I realized that locating Doctor Alexander Monro Tertius would prove difficult, perhaps impossible.

Mary, once we each were settled in private rooms in the same wealthy residence, suggested that I "think like Alex, John. Where would you be if you were stranded in Rome?"

"Hospital, clinic, private office," I said without hesitation. I smiled, "Or university."

"Exactly, John. Dr. Monro is a teacher."

We began our search, Percy and Claire joining us the second week after our arrival. Then, a week and half later, Claire announced that she had found an Alexander Monro in La Sapienza University of Rome. She reported that Monro appeared to be a lowly instructor of human anatomy, working long hours as he was also in charge of the cadaver laboratory, much as I had been at Edinburgh University.

We arranged to visit him, telling the university that we were interested in seeing their operations. When Monro first saw me, he immediately cried out, "I know you! You, I swear, ate a dead rat right in front of me. What? More than year ago now?"

I nodded, introduced myself, Mary and Percy Shelley and Lady Claire Byron. Then, I produced his wallet and leather satchel and attempted to hand them to the man, but the doctor was incredulous, raised his eyebrows, remarked, "You came all this way to return those? You easily could have posted them to me."

Mary explained, "We did not know where you were."

"So all four of you traveled to Rome to find me?" John nodded while Alexander continued, "What? To find me to return those?"

"Yes," said John, "and to apologize."

"For what?"

"I took your professorship at Edinburgh. I taught anatomy as you for one term this past year."

"As me?"

"I impersonated you, Doctor Monro."

The man was so shocked he did not seem capable of anger. Finally he asked, "How was that possible? You and I hardly appear as twins!"

"I cannot explain it," I lied, to be kind and to make this encounter easier on myself. I continued, "But I managed to fool many, both faculty and students. I have written to the Lord Provost and confessed. You may return to your home and take up your position at Edinburgh whenever you desire."

"You have lived in my father's house?"

"Yes, I live there now, but am prepared to vacate it at once."

Now, the man grew angry and his rage steadily rose to a height that did not frighten me, *not much frightens me now*, but Mary stepped back, fully expecting the doctor to attack. Not much goes as planned, so I said to Alexander, "We will take our leave now, good sir. Please try to forgive me. I will be out of your home as soon as I return to Scotland."

Doctor Monro spat, "You were just going to stay in my house if you did not locate me, were you not?"

I nodded, realizing this was the truth. I admitted that "yes, I was. I am sorry. I did not even think how utterly inappropriate that would have been. Please forgive me."

Although the lowly teacher remained angry, I could see that he was relaxing, his fist unfolding, his jaw going slack. He would not attack, he would not shout. Instead, as I anticipated, he began to sob. I said, pointing to the satchel which he finally took from me, "You will find that all the monies that were in your wallet the day you dropped it at my feet are there. You will find monies of mine as compensation for living in your home without your knowledge or permission. You also will find your updated travel documents and identification. Go to Scotland, sir."

He looked at Mary, Percy, and Claire, and then at me, said, "I will. Thank you."

Chapter Twenty-Four: Reconciliation

Once Mary and I returned to Edinburgh, which unsurprisingly required five weeks on two ships, we immediately set about the small task of moving me out of the 1 Great Stuart Street house in Charlotte Square. However, before I vacated the only place I had to live, I asked Mary to pen a letter, one of many she would pen for me over the following few days while we awaited Doctor Monro's homecoming.

Dear Mister and Mrs. Polidori,

I am writing the following letter for your son, John.

With kind regards, Mary Shelley

———

Dearest Mother and Father,

Once more, I must ask if I may come home for a while. I have found myself without a position and without a place to lay my head. I regret to inform you that I have been very ill, to the point of death. This horrible illness from which I am nearly recovered is why I am unable, at this time, to write legibly. My left hand shakes and of course it has never been the hand with which I would choose to write.

I await your reply to the postal office at Charlotte Square. Please address in care of Doctor John Polidori.

Your humble and loving son, John

When Mary finished listening to my dictation and began to fold the letter to place in an envelope, I saw that she had tears in her eyes. So did I, if I am honest. Weeping had apparently become my nature and I was not sure if I should be ashamed of myself. *Am I a man or a little boy?* I wondered.

✝

I had been away from Monro's house for nearly two and a half months. The post, wrapped in brown paper like it was a slab of meat, was placed on the front stoop, pressed against the front door. Therefore, that first day back, after dictating the letter to my parents, I sat at Monro's oak desk. Unfortunately, nearly all the post was addressed to me as Alexander with only a few envelopes addressed to me as John. I then used Monro's silver letter opener with my left hand and began to carefully slice into the envelopes by securing them to the surface of the desk with my right stump of a limb. Once I managed to open them, many were requests for payment which of course I would settle before my departure.

One in particular was addressed to Dr. John Polidori and was from the Lord Provost at Edinburgh University. I took it out of the envelope. The flimsy paper shook as I held it in my left hand, so I put it flat on the desk to read it. Like Alexander Monro in Rome, Sir William expressed in writing his incredulity, confusion, and anger. I decided, *I will ask Mary to pen a further apology.* I put his letter aside, then began to read the others. One in particular caught my eye because it was addressed to "Doctor John Monro." My heart skipped a beat. I called for Mary. She did not respond. I stood, yelled down the stairs as I believed she must have gone into the back kitchen. "Mary!"

"What?"

"Come up here to Alex's office, please!"

"Coming, John." Mary arrived in a timely manner. *She has always been a kind woman.* I showed her the envelope which I had left opened on the desk, but unread. I said, "Look how it is addressed."

Mary frowned initially, then a wide smile formed. For a moment, I felt as if one or the other was a faked response. But, she said cheerfully, "This letter, John *must* be from Cate."

"Exactly," I said, breathless. "No one else would refer to me as 'John Monro'!"

"Well, open it, silly."

"No, Mary. Please, you read it."

Mary poked me. "Coward."

I laughed. "I really am a coward, aren't I?"

She nodded, then said that she would read it first. She grew serious, and was apologetic for teasing me, saying "I understand your trepidation, John." Mary looked at the handwriting, commented, "You can tell Cate is a schoolmistress. Her penmanship is perfect. I think we should read this in the parlor where we can take our time."

I wondered what difference the parlor might make to the contents of Cate's letter, but I agreed, so we went down the staircase to the parlor. I sat across from my friend in an armchair while she sat on the sofa. Mary began to silently read the letter from Cate Ferguson. When she finished, Mary folded the paper, and handed me the letter. "You should read it, John." I studied her face, then unfolded what she had given to me, trusting that the words on the page would not be daggers to my heart.

Dearest John,

A nice woman who claimed to know you well, even better than I know you came almost nine months ago now and told me that you had been close to dying and that you have had a lengthy recovery. I was most shocked but also gratified, yes, I know that is horrid of me, to find out that you had a legitimate reason for your terrible silence and lengthy absence.

Then I saw a strange man with this woman, this friend of yours, sitting in a carriage much like one you and I liked to use. I especially thought the horse looked familiar, but unfortunately the man this woman claimed was you, did not. I was afraid. I admit that I am still afraid.

And so, after such a long delay and many arguments with myself, I have decided to ask you to visit whenever you are able to travel to Dean Village again. You need not write beforehand. You may come to my door, knock, and know that I will answer and let you in.

My fear, John, is that you will claim to be the strange man that sat on the seat next to the kind woman whose name I have forgotten. What I will do then only God knows.

Your loving Cate

I looked up at Mary, who nodded, said, "I know."

I asked her, "What do I do now?"

✝

Before Mary and I decided not to drive to Dean Village together, I completely vacated Alexander Monro Tertius' house. Most fortunately, as I explained to Mary when she saw what little I was taking with me, I had only the clothes on my back, my medical bag, and an empty wallet, therefore moving out proved quite easy to accomplish. I remarked almost flippantly, "As vampyre, Mary, I had little need of things."

"You had only *one* need."

"You are correct," I said, sadly recalling every human being I either had consumed by drinking blood or by murder outright.

Mary brightened, said, "Go on, John. Cate is waiting."

I smiled, confided, "I know how I will prove that I am the man she knows and loves."

Mary raised her eyebrows, asked, "How?"

"By telling her my horse *is* lonely."

Mary was puzzled, asked, "How will that work?"

"Once Cate commented to me," I explained, "that my horses were getting lonely, and I asked her if horses are capable of getting lonely. Cate said that of course horses can get lonely." I smiled at my friend.

Mary nodded, but said, "John, I have no doubts that you will be able to convince Cate that you are in fact the man she loves because you both shared so many special moments, but that is *not* your problem." She reached and placed her gloved hand atop mine, continued softly, "Your problem, John, is how are you to explain your complete change of appearance? When Cate met you, you looked like Alexander Monro, but now you look like yourself, like John Polidori. The only similarity is the loss of your right hand, and that, so far, has been unconvincing."

Immediately, I knew Mary was correct. I felt bewilderment, near devastation, then shook my head. I whispered, "I will *have to* tell her the truth."

"Yes, you will, and when you do, most likely Cate will react in the same way as Monro and the Lord Provost." She paused, then said, "probably much worse."

I finished Mary's thought, "Because she will *know* what I was when I kissed her and declared my love for her."

Mary nodded. "And Cate will be both afraid as she is now, and disgusted."

"She will know I lied to her," I said. I thought of the two times we had consummated our love. I whispered, "And defiled her."

Mary nodded again, even as she could not fully comprehend my second statement. She said, "John *this* is your problem."

I protested, "You *knew* this when you asked me to read her letter. You *knew* this. *Why* did you tell me to go to Cate?"

My dear friend looked away, then turned back to me, tears in her eyes as before, said, "Because Cate deserves to know the truth, John. She should be allowed to decide for herself whether she can forgive you, whether she is capable of trusting you again, whether she still loves you." *The dagger I thought might miss my heart strikes deep instead.* Mary added, "But I promise that if you need me, I will come with you, John and try to help Cate to see you and love you as I do."

I wept.

†

After wrestling with intense doubt, I decided that Mary Shelley should not accompany me to Dean Village. Mary agreed, and soon took the stagecoach for London so as to rejoin her husband, Percy. Mary and I had separately, also in union, realized that going to Cate was a task I had to do on my own. If I was going to tell Cate the truth, I was going to tell her the whole truth. And there were aspects of my time as vampyre that I had not told to Mary or Claire or anyone, aspects they would never *need* to know. But Cate, as Mary had wisely observed, deserved to know and needed to know the whole truth. I could not expect her to fall into my open arms again in ignorance of what I had been and what I had done as vampyre. She would need to know everything, including how I came to be the vampyre in the first place, how I lost my right hand and forearm, but worse than these horrors, Cate would need to be told how far I had descended into Darkness. She would need to be told how I murdered poor Beth Talbot in Soho, how I took both a whore's body and life, how I tore out the throats or drank the blood of many people unknown or unnamed to me, how I enslaved and nearly bled dry young Ross MacDonald, how I lied to and manipulated her, the woman I claimed to love. Yet Cate would also deserve as well as need to know how I was changed back to myself, how the glory of Heaven had literally conquered the powers of the witching hour in me. Not being a religious man, I nevertheless knew that I had been saved, quite literally by the name of Christ. As I struggled with my nearly overwhelming doubt as to whether I could win Cate back, I heard Claire's voice speaking *the words* over and over and over. As I tried to believe that Cate might forgive and love me again, Claire's sweet voice kept repeating the name of Jesus Christ, the name of the God I would never forget, and forever thank.

Epilogue

As of this sunny, yet cool summer day in the year of our Lord, 1821, Cate Ferguson is yet to forgive me. While I wait *in vain* for Cate's forgiveness, I struggle to compose my story, this book which I hope to finish before the sweltering days of August when I plan a return to my parents' home in Soho.

While I write with such poor legibility with my left hand, I recognize that Cate clearly is incapable of trusting this man, this John Polidori, who currently lives not far from her cottage, above the shop at the edge of Dean Village.

Despite this gulf between us, Cate talks to John, that is to me on infrequent occasions, usually in passing as we both purchase necessities in the shop below my little room. These brief encounters consist merely of polite formalities. I tip my top hat, murmur, "Good morning, Miss Ferguson," and a very few times she responds, "Good morning, Dr. Polidori." On even rarer occasions, Cate seeks my guidance as the village physician, primarily, of course because I am most convenient. Here, in my private office, her conversation with me is strictly professional. Finally, during the infrequent opportunities during which I attempt to approach Cate with simple words of kindness such as those that might occur between *former love interests,* Cate adamantly rebuffs me, insisting "we are not friends, Dr. Polidori." Oftentimes, Cate goes further, sharply telling me that she does not, cannot, and will not love me. Whereas I readily can accept that the young woman I continue to adore neither trusts nor forgives me, when Cate declares that she does not, cannot, and will not love me, I *try* not to believe her.

✝

To elucidate this unfortunate situation with Cate, allow me to digress. After moving out of the Monro house, I returned to my childhood home in Soho where, in late 1819, I published the story, *The Vampyre* which I had begun to write that terrible 1816 summer. Most strangely, Lord George Gordon Byron, my one time friend and sometime nemesis, initially received credit for it. I have recently attained both a retraction and correction from the publisher after George and Claire's kind assistance with Lord Byron emphatically denying that he "wrote *that!*" At the time, I laughed.

In early 1820, I returned to Edinburgh for a week to briefly visit with the Lord Provost at the university. I sought to verify that Doctor Alexander Monro Tertius had regained his teaching position. I was gratified to be told by the still angry Sir William that "yes, Doctor Monro has come back to us, thank God." He also assured me that the good doctor had returned to his home in Charlotte Square and found it "relatively intact."

Then, with apprehension, I asked about young Ross MacDonald. The Lord Provost responded that, after spending "a lengthy time of recovery" in Montrose Royal Lunatic Asylum suffering with "an unknown malady involving loss of blood that resulted in a form of insanity," the young student had indeed moved to Glasgow. The provost said, "As far as we know, Master MacDonald is performing well in his surgical studies at their medical college." Feeling only partially exonerated and minimally relieved, I thanked Sir William and took my leave.

While in Edinburgh, I wavered but finally decided to take a side trip to Dean Village where I hoped I would find the courage to approach the woman I loved. On a beautiful day, I leased a rig and single white horse. After reaching the small village, I stopped the carriage near the schoolhouse where I first met Margaret Catherine Ferguson as a vampyre impersonating Doctor Alexander Monro Tertius. Before I stepped down from the seat, I watched Cate as she corralled the elementary schoolchildren to apparently take them back into the white building for further instruction, perhaps in maths or grammar before the end of the school day.

Despite Cate's promise that she would allow me to speak with her, I remained hesitant. Finally I walked forward, attempting to gain her attention if ever so briefly without a wave or a shout. Cate turned when the white horse neighed loudly and stomped its left front hoof. She saw me, a strange man vaguely familiar *perhaps*. At this point, I raised my right stump in a kind of greeting. When she saw the short right limb, Cate stopped, turned toward me. As she abandoned her young charges to the playground to continue to walk rapidly in my direction, I moved toward her. As we neared one another, I called loudly, "Cate!"

"John?"

I nodded, but as she came closer, Cate failed to recognize my face which I had, of course, anticipated. I assured her, "Cate, it is I. I promise. I am John."

"How is that possible?"

"A long story, Cate."

Her utter confusion was evident in the expression on her soft, round face and in her robin egg blue eyes. She shook her head, her blondish curls catching the sunlight. Cate said, "Not more of this nonsense, I hope."

"Cate, it is not nonsense, but the truth I need to tell you. Please, meet me later at the watermill, the one you first showed to me. Please."

"Alone with you, a strange man. Nay sir, I think not."

I tried to say "the horse is lonely," but the words failed me. Our brief conversation ended as Cate turned away from me and went back to corralling the schoolchildren.

And so, my first conversation with Cate as a human being and of course as John Polidori proceeded somewhat as Mary Shelley had predicted and very much as I had feared.

†

After this failed attempt and several months back in Soho living with my parents, I decided to once again return to Scotland where I moved with my few belongings into a rented single room above the shop in Dean Village and began to function as the village physician, hanging my shingle outside the store.

While tending to the villagers, to their ills, their birthings and dyings, I waited for the right opportunity to talk with Cate a second time. This suitable moment proved to be nigh impossible because I *was* a coward as Mary and I had playfully recognized.

Despite a lack of resolution with Cate Ferguson, my life as a man, as a human being, and as a physician was settled finally.

†

After living in the village for several months, of course Miss Ferguson was aware of my presence. She neither sought me out nor particularly avoided me. Yet, we never spoke beyond the ordinary pleasantries that happen between strangers.

One afternoon, weary of this impasse, I gathered both my courage and my wits, rented a carriage, once again drawn by a single white horse, and met with Cate for our second conversation in Dean Village. True to her words in her earlier letter, when I knocked at her door unannounced, she allowed me, the village physician, whom she had already denied to be John Monro, into her cottage where she dutifully listened to me relate familiar aspects of her relationship with me as vampyre and the young man, Monro. All the while, she struggled to make sense of how two different men could be the same man.

As we sat across from one another at her dining table, Cate sipped her tea, her nerves causing her to pour in more cream as she listened. I watched her as she examined my eyes to see if she might recognize the John Monro she had known. Finally, after hearing me tell so many details which could only be known to the two of us, Cate whispered as she briefly touched my right sleeve pinned up at the elbow, "Romeo poisons his life for love of Juliet."

I nodded, said softly, "Yes, Cate, he does indeed."

Her blue eyes pierced mine as she asked the question I both dreaded and would be required to answer, "How is it that you are changed so, John?"

I took a deep breath because Cate had finally accepted that I was indeed the same man whom she had loved and who still loved her. I began to tell her the whole truth as I had planned. True to Mary Shelley's warning, Cate was immediately horrified, then she grew enraged.

Yes, she appreciated the power of blood lust and the enormous effort it had required of me to resist. And yes she, for a few moments at least, understood that the vampyre inside me, *the evil thing*, had been out of my control.

However, most unfortunately for Cate *and* for myself, we each quickly recognized that my inability, nay my difficulty in my control of the vampyre was *not* the entire truth.

As I told the whole truth to the woman I will love until I perish, I realized, despite being a lowly human being in the face of a power from Hell itself, that I had indeed gained control over the fiend. I remembered and admitted that I had been able to resist the blood scent of Claire as well as that of Cate, triumphs of self-control that a human being should not have been able to have over a vampyre. I knew in my heart that for over the span of two years and some months, I had kept the vampyre from taking the blood of children, and I had had the strength of will to keep it from killing Mary Shelley and the kind, though inept priest, Father McIntosh, and from enslaving Lady Claire Byron, its ultimate goal. And so, my culpability for *not* preventing the other horrors was plainly evident not only to me, but also to Cate.

Despite my apparent escape from Darkness, Cate and I each realized that *darkness resides in me.*

Cate stood up from her table, roughly pushed her tea from her while staring at me, *this thing* across from her. I could almost hear her thoughts. She said, "Get out, John."

I stood, nodded.

She continued, "You could have stopped it." Cate began to cry. She said, "What you did to Ross MacDonald, that unfortunate young man, that potential surgeon, is unforgivable, John. And that you drained Master MacDonald of his blood repeatedly supposedly so that you would not do the *same to me* is horrible to imagine and impossible to reconcile with goodness. You are *not* a decent man, John Polidori."

I nodded again.

Cate whispered, "You poor, pathetic, evil thing. You should have stopped it, John." She glared at me, "You should have taken your life, and thus, destroyed the vampyre." She stepped away from me. "I do not understand, John why you did not end the vampyre."

As Cate spoke, I recognized myself as *the evil thing.* I realized the truth, the whole truth as it emerged from the pure lips of this young woman I still loved. I wept.

Then Miss Ferguson, the schoolmistress of Dean Village, firmly, though not unkindly, turned me, John Polidori, the village physician, out of her cottage.

✝

The End

Obituary of John William Polidori

Born *7 September 1795* in Soho, City of Westminster, Greater London, England.

Took his own life by cyanide *14 August 1821* at the age of *25* in Soho, City of Westminster, Greater London, England.

Buried in St. Pancras Old Churchyard, Camden, Greater London, England in an unmarked grave.

Wake *17 August 1821*. In attendance: Gaetano and Anna Maria Polidori and John's siblings, and by his friends Percy Bysshe and Mary Wollstonecraft Godwin Shelley, Lady Claire Clairmont Byron, and Margaret Catherine Ferguson.

p. 147 was/is
p. 151 of course

ABOUT THE AUTHOR

Carley Eason Evans lives in the greater Charleston area, and has two grown children. She is a retired Medical Speech/Language Pathologist, having practiced primarily in acute care at the Medical University of South Carolina for twenty-five years.

Ms. Evans earned her Master of Science degree in Speech Language and Auditory Pathology from East Carolina University, Greenville, North Carolina in 1993; and her Bachelor of Arts degree in English/Writing from Denison University, Granville, Ohio in 1976 where she was elected to Mortar Board and Phi Beta Kappa.

Ms. Evans has published poems and short stories in a variety of small literary magazines. Currently, she has written and published eighteen novels via DooRFRame Books.

Other novels by Carley Eason Evans

Metal Man Walking

Annie Dreaming

In the Seventh Day (as Jane Cooper Easton)

The Eight-Foot Boy

After Jewel

Gani & Sean

The Only Thing

As From A Talented Animal

I Am Sofie

Gassed: A tale of the war to end all wars

Adam Immortal

38 Minutes

Boys Never Know

Burning the Red Candle

Incident at Silver Beach (formerly Silver Beach)

The Take-Back Girl

In a Grain of Sand, the Whole World

Made in United States
Orlando, FL
17 June 2025